William Makepeace Thackeray

Thackeray's Lighter Hours

William Makepeace Thackeray

Thackeray's Lighter Hours

ISBN/EAN: 9783337222314

Printed in Europe, USA, Canada, Australia, Japan

Cover: Foto ©Andreas Hilbeck / pixelio.de

More available books at **www.hansebooks.com**

Modern Classics

THACKERAY'S LIGHTER HOURS

BEING SELECTIONS FROM THE MINOR WRITINGS

OF

WILLIAM MAKEPEACE THACKERAY

BOSTON AND NEW YORK
HOUGHTON, MIFFLIN AND COMPANY
The Riverside Press, Cambridge

The Riverside Press, Cambridge, Mass., U. S. A.
Electrotyped and Printed by H. O. Houghton & Company.

CONTENTS.

DOCTOR BIRCH AND HIS YOUNG FRIENDS.

THE DOCTOR AND HIS STAFF.

THERE is no need to say why I became assistant-master and professor of the English and French languages, flower-painting, and the German flute, in Dr. Birch's Academy, at Rodwell Regis. Good folks may depend on this, that it was not for *choice* that I left lodgings near London, and a genteel society, for an under-master's desk in that old school. I promise you the fare at the usher's table, the getting up at five o'clock in the morning, the walking out with little boys in the fields (who used to play me tricks, and never could be got to respect my awful and responsible character as teacher in the school), Miss Birch's vulgar insolence, Jack Birch's glum condescension, and the poor old Doctor's patronage, were not matters in themselves pleasurable : and that that patronage and those dinners were

sometimes cruel hard to swallow. Never mind
— my connection with the place is over now,
and I hope they have got a more efficient under-master.

Jack Birch (Rev. J. Birch, of St. Neot's
Hall, Oxford) is partner with his father the
Doctor, and takes some of the classes. About
his Greek I can't say much; but I will construe
him in Latin any day. A more supercilious
little prig (giving himself airs, too, about his
cousin, Miss Raby, who lives with the Doctor),
a more empty, pompous little coxcomb I never
saw. His white neck - cloth looked as if it
choked him. He used to try and look over
that starch upon me and Prince the assistant,
as if we were a couple of footmen. He did n't
do much business in the school; but occupied
his time in writing sanctified letters to the boys'
parents, and in composing dreary sermons to
preach to them.

The real master of the school is Prince; an
Oxford man too; shy, haughty, and learned;
crammed with Greek and a quantity of useless
learning; uncommonly kind to the small boys;
pitiless with the fools and the braggarts; respected of all for his honesty, his learning, his
bravery (for he hit out once in a boat-row in a
way which astonished the boys and the barge-

men), and for a latent power about him, which all saw and confessed somehow. Jack Birch could never look him in the face. Old Miss Z. dared not put off any of *her* airs upon him. Miss Rosa made him the lowest of courtesies. Miss Raby said she was afraid of him. Good old Prince! we have sat many a night smoking in the Doctor's harness-room, whither we retired when our boys were gone to bed, and our cares and canes put by.

After Jack Birch had taken his degree at Oxford — a process which he effected with great difficulty — this place, which used to be called "Birch's," "Dr. Birch's Academy," and what not, became suddenly "Archbishop Wigsby's College of Rodwell Regis." They took down the old blue board with the gold letters, which has been used to mend the pigsty since. Birch had a large school-room run up in the Gothic taste, with statuettes, and a little belfry, and a bust of Archbishop Wigsby in the middle of the school. He put the six senior boys into caps and gowns, which had rather a good effect as the lads sauntered down the street of the town, but which certainly provoked the contempt and hostility of the bargemen; and so great was his rage for academic costumes and ordinances, that he would have put me myself into a lay gown, with red knots and fringes, but that I flatly resisted and said that a writing-master had no business with such paraphernalia.

By the way, I have forgotten to mention the Doctor himself. And what shall I say of him? Well, he has a very crisp gown and bands, a solemn aspect, a tremendous loud voice, and a grand air with the boys' parents; whom he receives in a study covered round with the best-bound books, which imposes upon many — upon the women especially — and makes them fancy that this is a Doctor indeed. But law bless you! He never reads the books, nor opens one of them; except that in which he keeps his bands — a Dugdale's "Monasticon," which looks like a book, but is in reality a cupboard, where he has his port, almond-cakes, and decanter of wine. He gets up his classics with translations, or what the boys call cribs; they pass wicked tricks upon him when he hears the forms. The elder wags go to his study and ask him to help them in hard bits of Herodotus or Thucydides; he says he will look over the passage, and flies for refuge to Mr. Prince, or to the crib. He keeps the flogging department in his own hands, finding that his son was too savage. He has awful brows and a big voice. But his roar frightens nobody. It is only a lion's skin; or, so to say, a muff.

Little Mordant made a picture of him with large ears, like a well-known domestic animal, and had his own justly boxed for the caricature. The Doctor discovered him in the fact, and was in a flaming rage, and threatened whipping at first; but in the course of the day an opportune basket of game arriving from Mordant's father, the Doctor became mollified, and has burnt the picture with the ears. However, I have one wafered up in my desk by the hand of the same little rascal.

THE COCK OF THE SCHOOL.

I am growing an old fellow, and have seen many great folks in the course of my travels and time : Louis Philippe coming out of the Tuileries ; his Majesty the King of Prussia and the Reichsverweser accolading each other at Cologne at my elbow ; Admiral Sir Charles Napier (in an omnibus once), the Duke of Wellington, the immortal Goethe at Weimar, the late benevolent Pope Gregory XVI., and a score more of the famous in this world — the whom whenever one looks at, one has a mild shock of awe and tremor. I like this feeling and decent fear and trembling with which a modest spirit salutes a Great Man.

Well, I have seen generals capering on horseback at the head of their crimson battalions;
bishops sailing down cathedral aisles, with
downcast eyes, pressing their trencher caps to
their hearts with their fat white hands; college
heads when her Majesty is on a visit; the
Doctor in all his glory at the head of his school
on speech-day; a great sight and all great men
these. I have never met the late Mr. Thomas
Cribb, but I have no doubt should have regarded
him with the same feeling of awe with which I
look every day at George Champion, the Cock
of Doctor Birch's school.

When, I say, I reflect as I go up and set him
a sum, that he could whop me in two minutes,
double up Prince and the other assistant, and
pitch the Doctor out of the window, I can't but
think how great, how generous, how magnanimous a creature this is that sits quite quiet and
good-natured, and works his equation, and
ponders through his Greek play. He might
take the school-room pillars and pull the house
down if he liked. He might close the door,
and demolish every one of us, like Antar, the
lover of Ibla; but he lets us live. He never
thrashes anybody without a cause; when woe
betide the tyrant or the sneak!

I think that to be strong and able to whop

everybody — not to do it, mind you, but to feel that you are able to do it — would be the greatest of all gifts. There is a serene good humor which plays about George Champion's broad face, which shows the consciousness of this power, and lights up his honest blue eyes with a magnanimous calm.

He is invictus. Even when a cub there was no beating this lion. Six years ago the undaunted little warrior actually stood up to Frank Davison (the Indian officer now — poor little Charley's brother, whom Miss Raby nursed so affectionately), — then seventeen years old, and the Cock of Birch's. They were obliged to drag off the boy, and Frank, with admiration and regard for him, prophesied the great things he would do. Legends of combats are preserved fondly in schools ; they have stories of such at Rodwell Regis, performed in the old Doctor's time, forty years ago.

Champion's affair with the Young Tutbury Pet, who was down here in training, — with Black the bargeman, — with the three head boys of Doctor Wapshot's academy, whom he caught maltreating an outlying day-boy of ours, etc., — are known to all the Rodwell Regis men. He was always victorious. He is modest and kind, like all great men. He has a good, brave, honest understanding. He cannot make verses like Young Pinder, or read Greek like Wells the Prefect, who is a perfect young abyss of learning, and knows enough, Prince says, to furnish any six first-class men ; but he does his work in a sound, downright way, and he is made to be the bravest of soldiers, the best of country parsons, an honest English gentleman wherever he may go.

Old Champion's chief friend and attendant is Young Jack Hall, whom he saved, when drowning, out of the Miller's Pool. The attachment of the two is curious to witness. The smaller lad gamboling, playing tricks round the bigger one, and perpetually making fun of his protector. They are never far apart, and of holidays you may meet them miles away from the school, — George sauntering heavily down the lanes with his big stick, and little Jack larking with the pretty girls in the cottage windows.

George has a boat on the river, in which, however, he commonly lies smoking, whilst Jack sculls him. He does not play at cricket, except when the school plays the county or at Lord's in the holidays. The boys can't stand his bowling, and when he hits, it is like trying to catch a cannon-ball. I have seen him at tennis. It is a splendid sight to behold the young fellow bounding over the court with streaming yellow hair, like young Apollo in a flannel jacket.

The other head boys are Lawrence, the captain; Bunce, famous chiefly for his magnificent appetite; and Pitman, surnamed Roscius, for his love of the drama. Add to these Swanky, called Macassar, from his partiality to that condiment, and who has varnished boots, wears white gloves on Sundays, and looks out for Miss Pinkerton's school (transferred from Chiswick to Rodwell Regis, and conducted by the nieces of the late Miss Barbara Pinkerton, the friend of our great lexicographer, upon the principles approved by him, and practiced by that admirable woman) as it passes into church.

Representations have been made concerning Mr. Horace Swanky's behavior; rumors have been uttered about notes in verse, conveyed in three - cornered puffs, by Mrs. Ruggles, who serves Miss Pinkerton's young ladies on Fridays, — and how Miss Didow, to whom the tart and inclosure were addressed, tried to make away with herself by swallowing a ball of cotton. But I pass over these absurd reports, as likely to affect the reputation of an admirable seminary conducted by irreproachable females. As they go into church, Miss P. driving in her

flock of lambkins with the crook of her parasol,
how can it be helped if her forces and ours
sometimes collide, as the boys are on their way
up to the organ-loft? And I don't believe a
word about the three-cornered puff, but rather
that it was the invention of that jealous Miss
Birch, who is jealous of Miss Raby, jealous of
everybody who is good and handsome, and who
has *her own ends* in view, or I am very much in
error.

THE DEAR BROTHERS.

A MELODRAMA IN SEVERAL ROUNDS.

THE DOCTOR.
MR. TIPPER, Uncle to the Masters Boxall.
BOXALL MAJOR, BOXALL MINOR, BROWN, JONES,
SMITH, ROBINSON, TIFFIN MINIMUS.

B. Go it, old Boxall!
J. Give it him, young Boxall!
R. Pitch into him, old Boxall!
S. Two to one on young Boxall!

Enter TIFFIN MINIMUS, *running.*

Tiffin Minimus. — Boxalls! you're wanted.
(*The Doctor to Mr. Tipper.*) — Every boy in
the school loves them, my dear sir; your

nephews are a credit to my establishment.
They are orderly, well-conducted, gentleman-
like boys. Let us enter and find them at their
studies.

Enter The DOCTOR *and* Mr. TIPPER.

GRAND TABLEAU.

THE LITTLE SCHOOL-ROOM.

WHAT they call the little school-room is a
small room at the other end of the great
school ; through which you go to the Doctor's
private house, and where Miss Raby sits with
her pupils. She has a half-dozen very small
ones over whom she presides and teaches them
in her simple way, until they are big or learned
enough to face the great school-room. Many
of them are in a hurry for promotion, the grace-
less little simpletons, and know no more than
their elders when they are well off.

She keeps the accounts, writes out the bills,
superintends the linen, and sews on the general
shirt-buttons. Think of having such a woman
at home to sew on one's shirt-buttons ! But
peace, peace, thou foolish heart !

Miss Raby is the Doctor's niece. Her mother
was a beauty (quite unlike old Zoe therefore) ;

and she married a pupil in the old Doctor's time, who was killed afterwards, a captain in the East India service, at the siege of Bhurtpore. Hence a number of Indian children come to the Doctor's ; for Raby was very much liked, and the uncle's kind reception of the orphan has been a good speculation for the school-keeper.

It is wonderful how brightly and gayly that little quick creature does her duty. She is the first to rise, and the last to sleep, if any business is to be done. She sees the other two women go off to parties in the town without even so much as wishing to join them. It is Cinderella, only contented to stay at home — content to bear Zoe's scorn and to admit Rosa's superior charms — and to do her utmost to repay her uncle for his great kindness in housing her.

So you see she works as much as three maid-servants for the wages of one. She is as thankful when the Doctor gives her a new gown, as if he had presented her with a fortune ; laughs at his stories most good-humoredly, listens to Zoe's scolding most meekly, admires Rosa with all her heart, and only goes out of the way when Jack Birch shows his sallow face ; for she can't bear him, and always finds work when he comes near.

How different she is when some folks approach her! I won't be presumptuous; but I think, I think, I have made a not unfavorable impression in some quarters. However, let us be mum on this subject. I like to see her, because she always looks good-humored : because she is always kind, because she is always modest, because she is fond of those poor little brats — orphans some of them, — because she is rather ' pretty, I dare say, or because I think so, which comes to the same thing.

Though she is kind to all, it must be owned she shows the most gross favoritism towards the amiable children. She brings them cakes from dessert, and regales them with Zoe's preserves ; spends many of her little shillings in presents for her favorites, and will tell them stories by the hour. She has one very sad story about a little boy who died long ago : the younger children are never weary of hearing about him ; and Miss Raby has shown to one of them a lock of the little chap's hair, which she keeps in her work-box to this day.

A HOPELESS CASE.

LET us, people who are so uncommonly clever and learned, have a great tenderness and pity for the poor folks who are not endowed with the prodigious talents which we have. I have always had a regard for dunces ; — those of my own school-days were amongst the pleasantest of the fellows, and have turned out by no means the dullest in life ; whereas many a youth who could turn off Latin hexameters by the yard, and construe Greek quite glibly, is no better 'than a feeble prig now, with not a pennyworth more brains than were in his head before his beard grew.

Those poor dunces ! Talk of being the last man, ah ! what a pang it must be to be the last boy — huge, misshapen, fourteen years of age, and "taken up" by a chap who is but six years old, and can't speak quite plain yet !

Master Hulker is in that condition at Birch's. He is the most honest, kind, active, plucky, generous creature. He can do many things better than most boys. He can go up a tree, pump, play at cricket, dive and swim perfectly — he can eat twice as much as almost any lady (as Miss Birch well knows), he has a pretty talent at carving figures with his hack-knife, he makes and paints little coaches, he can take a watch to pieces and put it together again. He can do everything but learn his lessons ; and then he sticks at the bottom of the school hopeless. As the little boys are drafted in from Miss Raby's class (it is true she is one of the best instructresses in the world), they enter and hop over poor Hulker. He would be handed over to the governess, only he is too big. Sometimes I used to think that this desperate stupidity was a stratagem of the poor rascal's, and that he shammed dullness, so that he might be degraded into Miss Raby's class — if she would teach *me*, I know, before George, I would put on a pinafore and a little jacket — but no, it is a natural incapacity for the Latin Grammar.

If you could see his grammar, it is a perfect curiosity of dog's ears. The leaves and cover are all curled and ragged. Many of the pages are worn away with the rubbing of his elbows as he sits poring over the hopeless volume, with the blows of his fists as he thumps it madly, or with the poor fellow's tears. You see him wiping them away with the back of his hand, as he tries and tries, and can't do it.

When I think of that Latin Grammar, and that infernal As in præsenti, and of other things which I was made to learn in my youth, upon my conscience, I am surprised that we ever survived it. When one thinks of the boys who have been caned because they could not master that intolerable jargon ! Good Lord,

what a pitiful chorus these poor little creatures
send up ! Be gentle with them, ye schoolmasters, and only whop those who *won't* learn.

The Doctor has operated upon Hulker (between ourselves), but the boy was so little affected you would have thought he had taken
chloroform. Birch is weary of whipping now,
and leaves the boy to go his own gait. Prince,
when he hears the lesson, and who cannot help
making fun of a fool, adopts the sarcastic manner with Master Hulker, and says, " Mr. Hulker,
may I take the liberty to inquire if your brilliant intellect has enabled you to perceive the
difference between those words which gramma-
rians have defined as substantive and adjective
nouns ? if not, perhaps Mr. Ferdinand Timmins
will instruct you." And Timmins hops over
Hulker's head.

I wish Prince would leave off girding at the
poor lad. He is a boy, and his mother is a
widow woman, who loves him with all her
might. There is a famous sneer about the
suckling of fools and the chronicling of small
beer ; but remember it was a rascal who uttered it.

A WORD ABOUT MISS BIRCH.

"THE gentlemen, and especially the younger and more tender of these pupils, will have the advantage of the constant superintendence and affectionate care of Miss Zoe Birch, sister of the principal, whose dearest aim will be to supply (as far as may be) the absent maternal friend." — *Prospectus of Rodwell Regis School.*

This is all very well in the Doctor's prospectus, and Miss Zoe Birch — (a pretty blossom it is, fifty-five years old, during two score of which she has dosed herself with pills ; with a nose as red and a face as sour as a crab-apple) — this is all mighty well in a prospectus. But I should like to know who would take Miss Zoe for a mother, or would have her for one ?

The only persons in the house who are not afraid of her are Miss Rosa and I — no, I am afraid of her, though I *do* know the story about the French usher in 1830 — but all the rest tremble before the woman, from the Doctor down to poor Francis, the knife-boy, whom she bullies into his miserable blacking-hole.

The Doctor is a pompous and outwardly severe man — but inwardly weak and easy ; loving a joke and a glass of port-wine. I get on with him, therefore, much better than Mr. Prince, who scorns him for an ass, and under whose keen eyes the worthy Doctor writhes like a convicted impostor; and many a sunshiny afternoon would he have said, "Mr. T., sir, shall we try another glass of that yellow sealed wine which you seem to like?" (and which he likes even better than I do) had not the old harridan of a Zoe been down upon us, and insisted on turning me out with her abominable weak coffee. She a mother, indeed! A sour-milk generation she would have nursed. She is always croaking, scolding, bullying — yowling at the housemaids, snarling at Miss Raby, bowwowing after the little boys, barking after the big ones. She knows how much every boy eats to an ounce; and her delight is to ply with fat the little ones who can't bear it, and with raw meat those who hate underdone. It was she who caused the Doctor to be eaten out three times; and nearly created a rebellion in the school because she insisted on his flogging Goliath Longman.

The only time that woman is happy is when she comes in of a morning to the little boys' dormitories with a cup of hot Epsom salts, and a sippet of bread. Boo! — the very notion makes me quiver. She stands over them. I saw her do it to young Byles only a few days since ; and her presence makes the abomination doubly abominable.

As for attending them in real illness, do you suppose that she would watch a single night for any one of them? Not she. When poor little Charley Davison (that child a lock of whose soft hair I have said how Miss Raby still keeps) lay ill of scarlet fever in the holidays — for the Colonel, the father of these boys, was in India — it was Anne Raby who tended the child, who watched him all through the fever, who never left him while it lasted, or until she had closed the little eyes that were never to brighten or moisten more. Anne watched and deplored him ; but it was Miss Birch who wrote the letter announcing his demise, and got the gold chain and locket which the Colonel ordered as a memento of his gratitude. It was through a row with Miss Birch that Frank Davison ran away. I promise you that after he joined his regiment in India, the Ahmednuggur Irregulars, which his gallant father commands, there came over no more annual shawls and presents to Dr. and Miss Birch ; and that if she fancied the Colonel was coming home to marry her (on account of her tenderness to his motherless children, which he was always writing about), *that* notion was very soon given up. But these affairs are of early date, seven years back, and I only heard of them in a very confused manner from Miss Raby, who was a girl, and had just come to Rodwell Regis. She is always very much moved when she speaks about those boys ; which is but seldom. I take it the death of the little one still grieves her tender heart.

Yes, it is Miss Birch who has turned away seventeen ushers and second-masters in eleven years, and half as many French masters, I suppose, since the departure of her *favorite*, M. Grinche, with her gold watch, etc. ; but this is only surmise — that is, from hearsay, and from Miss Rosa taunting her aunt, as she does sometimes, in her graceful way ; but besides this, I have another way of keeping her in order.

Whenever she is particularly odious or insolent to Miss Raby, I have but to introduce raspberry jam into the conversation, and the woman holds her tongue. She will understand me. I need not say more.

NOTE, 12*th December*. — I *may* speak now. I have left the place and don't mind. I say then at once, and without caring twopence for the consequences, that I saw this woman, this *mother* of the boys, EATING JAM WITH A SPOON

OUT OF MASTER WIGGINS'S TRUNK IN THE BOX-ROOM : and of this I am ready to take an affidavit any day.

A TRAGEDY.

THE DRAMA OUGHT TO BE REPRESENTED IN ABOUT SIX ACTS.

[*The school is hushed.* LAWRENCE *the Prefect, and Custos of the rods, is marching after the* DOCTOR *into the operating-room.* MASTER BACKHOUSE *is about to follow.*]

Master Backhouse. — It's all very well, but you see if I don't pay you out after school — you sneak you !

Master Lurcher. — If you do I 'll tell again.

[*Exit* BACKHOUSE.

[*The rod is heard from the adjoining apartment. Hwish — hwish — hwish — hwish — hwish — hwish — hwish !*

Re-enter BACKHOUSE.

BRIGGS IN LUCK.

Enter the Knife-boy. — Hamper for Briggses !
Master Brown. — Hurray, Tom Briggs ! I 'll
lend you my knife.

————

IF this story does not carry its own moral,
what fable does, I wonder ? Before the arrival
of that hamper, Master Briggs was in no better
repute than any other young gentleman of the
lower school ; and in fact I had occasion myself, only lately, to correct Master Brown for
kicking his friend's shins during the writing-
lesson. But how this basket, directed by his
mother's housekeeper and marked "Glass with
care " (whence I conclude that it contains some
jam and some bottles of wine, probably, as well
as the usual cake and game-pie, and half a
sovereign for the elder Master B., and five new
shillings for Master Decimus Briggs) — how, I
say, the arrival of this basket alters all Master
Briggs's circumstances in life, and the estimation in which many persons regard him !

If he is a good-hearted boy, as I have reason
to think, the very first thing he will do, before
inspecting the contents of the hamper, or cutting into them with the knife which Master

Brown has so considerately lent him, will be to
read over the letter from home which lies on
the top of the parcel. He does so, as I remark
to Miss Raby (for whom I happen to be mending pens when the little circumstance arose),
with a flushed face and winking eyes. Look
how the other boys are peering into the basket as he reads. — I say to her, "Isn't it a
pretty picture?" Part of the letter is in a
very large hand. This is from his little sister.
And I would wager that she netted the little
purse which he has just taken out of it, and
which Master Lynx is eying.

"You are a droll man, and remark all sorts
of queer things," Miss Raby says, smiling, and
plying her swift needle and fingers as quick as
possible.

"I am glad we are both on the spot, and that
the little fellow lies under our guns as it were,
and so is protected from some such brutal
school-pirate as young Duval for instance, who
would rob him, probably, of some of those good
things ; good in themselves, and better because
fresh from home. See, there is a pie as I said,
and which I dare say is better than those which
are served at our table (but you never take any
notice of such kind of things, Miss Raby), a
cake of course, a bottle of currant-wine, jam-

pots, and no end of pears in the straw. With
their money little Briggs will be able to pay
the tick which that imprudent child has run up
with Mrs. Ruggles ; and I shall let Briggs
Major pay for the pencil-case which Bullock
sold to him. — It will be a lesson to the young
prodigal for the future. But I say, what a
change there will be in his life for some time
to come, and at least until his present wealth is
spent ! The boys who bully him will mollify
towards him, and accept his pie and sweetmeats. They will have feasts in the bedroom;
and that wine will taste more delicious to them
than the best out of the Doctor's cellar. The
cronies will be invited. Young Master Wagg
will tell his most dreadful story and sing his
best song for a slice of that pie. What a jolly
night they will have ! When we go the rounds
at night, Mr. Prince and I will take care to
make a noise before we come to Briggs's room,
so that the boys may have time to put the light
out, to push the things away, and to scud into
bed. Doctor Spry may be put in requisition
the next morning."

"Nonsense ! you absurd creature," cries out
Miss Raby, laughing ; and I lay down the
twelfth pen very nicely mended.

" Yes ; after luxury comes the doctor, I say ;

after extravagance a hole in the breeches pocket. To judge from his disposition, Briggs Major will not be much better off a couple of days hence than he is now; and, if I am not mistaken, will end life a poor man. Brown will be kicking his shins before a week is over, depend upon it. There are boys and men of all sorts, Miss R. — There are selfish sneaks who hoard until the store they dare n't use grows mouldy — there are spendthrifts who fling away, parasites who flatter and lick its shoes, and snarling curs who hate and envy, good fortune."

I put down the last of the pens, brushing away with it the quill-chips from her desk first, and she looked at me with a kind, wondering face. I brushed them away, clicked the penknife into my pocket, made her a bow, and walked off — for the bell was ringing for school.

A YOUNG FELLOW WHO IS PRETTY SURE TO SUCCEED.

If Master Briggs is destined in all probability to be a poor man, the chances are that Mr. Bullock will have a very different lot. He is a son of a partner of the eminent banking firm of

Bullock and Hulker, Lombard Street, and very high in the upper school — quite out of my jurisdiction, consequently.

He writes the most beautiful current-hand ever seen ; and the way in which he mastered arithmetic (going away into recondite and wonderful rules in the Tutor's Assistant, which some masters even dare not approach) is described by the Doctor in terms of admiration. He is Mr. Prince's best algebra pupil ; and a very fair classic, too ; doing everything well for which he has a mind.

He does not busy himself with the sports of his comrades, and holds a cricket-bat no better than Miss Raby would. He employs the play-hours in improving his mind, and reading the newspaper ; he is a profound politician, and, it must be owned, on the liberal side. The elder boys despise him rather ; and when Champion Major passes, he turns his head, and looks down. I don't like the expression of Bullock's narrow green eyes, as they follow the elder Champion, who does not seem to know or care how much the other hates him.

No. Mr. Bullock, though perhaps the cleverest and most accomplished boy in the school, associates with the quite little boys when he is minded for society. To these he is quite affable,

courteous, and winning. He never fagged or
thrashed one of them. He has done the verses
and corrected the exercises of many, and many
is the little lad to whom he has lent a little
money.

It is true he charges at the rate of a penny a
week for every sixpence lent out ; but many a
fellow to whom tarts are a present necessity is
happy to pay this interest for the loan. These
transactions are kept secret. Mr. Bullock, in
rather a whining tone, when he takes Master
Green aside and does the requisite business for
him, says, " You know you 'll go and talk about
it everywhere. I don't want to lend you the
money, I want to buy something with it. It 's
only to oblige you ; and yet I am sure you will
go and make fun of me." Whereon, of course,
Green, eager for the money, vows solemnly
that the transaction shall be confidential, and
only speaks when the payment of the interest
becomes oppressive.

Thus it is that Mr. Bullock's practices are at
all known. At a very early period, indeed, his
commercial genius manifested itself : and by
happy speculations in toffey ; by composing a
sweet drink made of stick-liquorice and brown
sugar, and selling it at a profit to the younger
children ; by purchasing a series of novels,

which he let out at an adequate remuneration ; by doing boys' exercises for a penny, and other processes, he showed the bent of his mind. At the end of the half-year he always went home richer than when he arrived at school, with his purse full of money.

Nobody knows how much he brought ; but the accounts are fabulous. Twenty, thirty, fifty — it is impossible to say how many sovereigns. When joked about his money, he turns pale and swears he has not a shilling ; whereas he has had a banker's account ever since he was thirteen.

At the present moment he is employed in negotiating the sale of a knife with Master Green, and is pointing out to the latter the beauty of the six blades, and that he need not pay until after the holidays.

Champion Major has sworn that he will break every bone in his skin the next time that he cheats a little boy, and is bearing down upon him. Let us come away. It is frightful to see that big peaceful clever coward moaning under well-deserved blows and whining for mercy.

DUVAL THE PIRATE.

JONES MINIMUS *passes laden with tarts.*

Duval.—Hullo! you small boy with the tarts! Come here, sir.

Jones Minimus.—Please, Duval, they ain't mine.

Duval.—Oh, you abominable young story-teller.   [*He confiscates the goods.*

I think I like young Duval's mode of levying contributions better than Bullock's. The former's, at least, has the merit of more candor. Duval is the pirate of Birch's, and lies in wait for small boys laden with money or provender. He scents plunder from afar off, and pounces out on it. Woe betide the little fellow when Duval boards him!

There was a youth here whose money I used to keep, as he was of an extravagant and weak taste; and I doled it out to him in weekly shillings, sufficient for the purchase of the necessary tarts. This boy came to me one day for half a sovereign, for a very particular purpose, he said. I afterwards found he wanted to lend the money to Duval.

The young ogre burst out laughing, when in a great wrath and fury I ordered him to refund to the little boy, and proposed a bill of exchange at three months. It is true Duval's father does not pay the Doctor, and the lad never has a shilling, save that which he levies; and though he is always bragging about the splendor of Freenystown, Co. Cork, and the fox-hounds his father keeps, and the claret they drink there—there comes no remittance from Castle Freeny in these bad times to the honest Doctor; who is a kindly man enough, and never yet turned an insolvent boy out of doors.

THE DORMITORIES.

MASTER HEWLETT AND MASTER NIGHTINGALE.

(Rather a cold winter night.)

Hewlett (flinging a shoe at Master Nightingale's bed, with which he hits that young gentleman). — Hullo, you! Get up and bring me that shoe!

Nightingale. — Yes, Hewlett. *(He gets up.)*

Hewlett. — Don't drop it, and be very careful of it, sir.

Nightingale. — Yes, Hewlett.

Hewlett. — Silence in the dormitory! Any

boy who opens his mouth, I'll murder him.
Now, sir, are not you the boy what can sing?

Nightingale. — Yes, Hewlett.

Hewlett. — Chant, then, till I go to sleep, and
if I wake when you stop, you 'll have this at
your head.

[MASTER HEWLETT *lays his Bluchers on the
bed, ready to shy at Master Nightingale's
head in the case contemplated.*

Nightingale (timidly). — Please, Hewlett?

Hewlett. — Well, sir?

Nightingale. — May I put on my trousers,
please?

Hewlett. — *No,* sir. Go on, or I'll —

Nightingale. —

" Through pleasures and palaces
    Though we may roam,
Be it ever so humble,
    There 's no place like home."

A CAPTURE AND A RESCUE.

MY young friend, Patrick Champion, George's
younger brother, a late arrival among us ; has
much of the family quality and good nature ;
is not in the least a tyrant to the small boys,
but is as eager as Amadis to fight. He is box-
ing his way up the school, emulating his great

brother. He fixes his eye on a boy above him in strength or size, and you hear somehow that a difference has arisen between them at football, and they have their coats off presently. He has thrashed himself over the heads of many youths in this manner : for instance, if Champion can lick Dobson, who can thrash Hobson, how much more, then, can he thrash Hobson ? Thus he works up and establishes his position in the school. Nor does Mr. Prince think it advisable that we ushers should walk much in the way when these little differences are being settled, unless there is some gross disparity, or danger is apprehended.

For instance, I own to having seen this row as I was shaving at my bedroom window. I did not hasten down to prevent its consequences. Fogle had confiscated a top, the property of Snivins ; the which, as the little wretch was always pegging it at my toes, I did not regret. Snivins whimpered ; and young Champion came up, lusting for battle. Directly he made out Fogle, he steered for him, pulling up his coat-sleeves, and clearing for action.

" Who spoke to *you*, young Champion ? " Fogle said, and he flung down the top to Master Snivins. I knew there would be no fight ; and perhaps Champion, too, was disappointed.

THE GARDEN.

WHERE THE PARLOR-BOARDERS GO.

NOBLEMEN have been rather scarce at Birch's
— but the heir of a great Prince has been living
with the Doctor for some years. — He is Lord
George Gaunt's eldest son, the noble Plantagenet Gaunt Gaunt, and nephew of the Most
Honorable the Marquis of Steyne.

They are very proud of him at the Doctor's
— and the two Misses and Papa, whenever a
stranger comes down whom they want to dazzle,
are pretty sure to bring Lord Steyne into the
conversation, mention the last party at Gaunt
House, and cursorily to remark that they have
with them a young friend who will be, in all
human probability, Marquis of Steyne and
Earl of Gaunt, etc.

Plantagenet does not care much about these
future honors ; provided he can get some brown
sugar on his bread and butter, or sit with three
chairs and play at coach-and-horses quite quietly
by himself, he is tolerably happy. He saunters
in and out of school when he likes, and looks at
the masters and other boys with a listless grin.
He used to be taken to church, but he laughed

and talked in odd places, so they are forced to leave him at home now. He will sit with a bit of string and play cat's-cradle for many hours. He likes to go and join the very small children at their games. Some are frightened at him; but they soon cease to fear, and order him about. I have seen him go and fetch tarts from Mrs. Ruggles for a boy of eight years old; and cry bitterly if he did not get a piece. He cannot speak quite plain, but very nearly; and is not more, I suppose, than three-and-twenty.

Of course at home they know his age, though they never come and see him. But they forget that Miss Rosa Birch is no longer a young chit as she was ten years ago, when Gaunt was brought to the school. On the contrary, she has had no small experience in the tender passion, and is at this moment smitten with a disinterested affection for Plantagenet Gaunt.

Next to a little doll with a burnt nose, which he hides away in cunning places, Mr. Gaunt is very fond of Miss Rosa too. What a pretty match it would make! and how pleased they would be at Gaunt House, if the grandson and heir of the great Marquis of Steyne, the descendant of a hundred Gaunts and Tudors, should marry Miss Birch, the schoolmaster's daughter! It is true she has the sense on her

side, and poor Plantagenet is only an idiot ; but
there he is, a zany, with such expectations and
such a pedigree !

If Miss Rosa would run away with Mr.
Gaunt, she would leave off bullying her cousin,
Miss Anne Raby. Shall I put her up to the
notion, and offer to lend her money to run
away ? Mr. Gaunt is not allowed money. He
had some once, but Bullock took him into a
corner, and got it from him. He has a moderate tick opened at a tart-woman's. He stops
at Rodwell Regis through the year : school-
time and holiday-time, it is all the same to him.
Nobody asks about him, or thinks about him,
save twice a year, when the Doctor goes to
Gaunt House, and gets the amount of his bills,
and a glass of wine in the steward's room.

And yet you see somehow that he is a gentleman. His manner is different to that of the
owners of that coarse table and parlor at which
he is a boarder (I do not speak of Miss R. of
course, for *her* manners are as good as those of
a duchess). When he caught Miss Rosa box-
ing little Fiddes's ears, his face grew red, and
he broke into a fierce inarticulate rage. After
that, and for some days, he used to shrink from
her ; but they are reconciled now. I saw them
this afternoon in the garden where only the

parlor-boarders walk. He was playful, and
touched her with his stick. She raised her
handsome eyes in surprise, and smiled on him
very kindly.

The thing was so clear, that I thought it my
duty to speak to old Zoe about it. The wicked
old catamaran told me she wished that some
people would mind their own business, and hold
their tongues — that some persons were paid to
teach writing, and not to tell tales and make
mischief : and I have since been thinking
whether I ought to communicate with the
Doctor.

THE OLD PUPIL

As I came into the playgrounds this morning,
I saw a dashing young fellow, with a tanned
face and a blonde moustache, who was walking
up and down the green arm-in-arm with Champion Major, and followed by a little crowd of
boys.

They were talking of old times evidently.
" What had become of Irvine and Smith ? " —
" Where was Bill Harris and Jones : not Squinny
Jones, but Cocky Jones ? " — and so forth.
The gentleman was no stranger ; he was an
old pupil evidently, come to see if any of his

old comrades remained, and revisit the *cari luoghi* of his youth.

Champion was evidently proud of his arm-fellow. He espied his brother, young Champion, and introduced him. "Come here, sir," he called. "The young 'un was n't here in your time, Davison." "Pat, sir," said he, "this is Captain Davison, one of Birch's boys. Ask him who was among the first in the lines at Sobraon?"

Pat's face kindled up as he looked Davison full in the face and held out his hand. Old Champion and Davison both blushed. The infantry set up a "Hurray, hurray, hurray," Champion leading, and waving his wide-awake. I protest that the scene did one good to witness. Here was the hero and cock of the school come back to see his old haunts and cronies. He had always remembered them. Since he had seen them last, he had faced death and achieved honor. But for my dignity I would have shied up my hat too.

With a resolute step, and his arm still linked in Champion's, Captain Davison now advanced, followed by a wake of little boys, to that corner of the green where Mrs. Ruggles has her tart stand.

"Hullo, Mother Ruggles! don't you remember me?" he said, and shook her by the hand.

"Lor, if it ain't Davison Major!" she said. "Well, Davison Major, you owe me fourpence for two sausage-rolls from when you went away."

Davison laughed, and all the little crew of boys set up a similar chorus.

"I buy the whole shop," he said. "Now, young 'uns — eat away!"

Then there was such a "Hurray! hurray!" as surpassed the former cheer in loudness. Everybody engaged in it except Piggy Duff, who made an instant dash at the three-cornered puffs, but was stopped by Champion, who said there should be a fair distribution. And so there was, and no one lacked, neither of raspberry, open tarts, nor of mellifluous bull's eyes, nor of polonies, beautiful to the sight and taste.

The hurraying brought out the old Doctor himself, who put his hand up to his spectacles and started when he saw the old pupil. Each blushed when he recognized the other; for seven years ago they had parted not good friends.

"What — Davison?" the Doctor said, with a tremulous voice. "God bless you, my dear fellow!" — and they shook hands. "A half-holiday, of course, boys," he added, and there was another hurray : there was to be no end to the cheering that day.

"How 's — how 's the family, sir ? " Captain Davison asked.

"Come in and see. Rosa's grown quite a lady. Dine with us, of course. Champion Major, come to dinner at five. Mr. Titmarsh, the pleasure of your company ? " The Doctor swung open the garden gate : the old master and pupil entered the house reconciled.

I thought I would first peep into Miss Raby's room, and tell her of this event. She was working away at her linen there, as usual quiet and cheerful.

"You should put up," I said with a smile ; "the Doctor has given us a half-holiday."

"I never have holidays," Miss Raby replied.

Then I told her of the scene I had just witnessed, of the arrival of the old pupil, the purchase of the tarts, the proclamation of the holiday, and the shouts of the boys of "Hurray, Davison ! "

"*Who* is it ? " cried out Miss Raby, starting and turning as white as a sheet.

I told her it was Captain Davison from India ; and described the appearance and behavior of the Captain. When I had finished speaking, she asked me to go and get her a glass of water ; she felt unwell. But she was gone when I came back with the water.

I know all now. After sitting for a quarter of an hour with the Doctor, who attributed his guest's uneasiness no doubt to his desire to see Miss Rosa Birch, Davison started up and said he wanted to see Miss Raby. "You remember, sir, how kind she was to my little brother, sir ?" he said. Whereupon the Doctor, with a look of surprise, that anybody should want to see Miss Raby, said she was in the little school-room ; whither the Captain went, knowing the way from old times.

A few minutes afterwards, Miss R. and Miss Z. returned from a drive with Plantagenet Gaunt in their one-horse fly, and being informed of Davison's arrival, and that he was closeted with Miss Raby in the little school-room, of course made for that apartment at once. I was coming into it from the other door. I wanted to know whether she had drunk the water.

This is what both parties saw. The two were in this very attitude. "Well, upon my word !" cries out Miss Zoe ; but Davison did not let go his hold ; and Miss Raby's head only sank down on his hand.

"You must get another governess, sir, for the little boys," Frank Davison said to the Doctor. "Anne Raby has promised to come with me."

You may suppose I shut to the door on my side. And when I returned to the little school-room, it was black and empty. Everybody was gone. I could hear the boys shouting at play in the green outside. The glass of water was on the table where I had placed it. I took it and drank it myself, to the health of Anne Raby and her husband. It was rather a choker.

But of course I was n't going to stop on at Birch's. When his young friends reassemble on the 1st of February next, they will have two new masters. Prince resigned too, and is at present living with me at my old lodgings at Mrs. Cammysole's. If any nobleman or gentleman wants a private tutor for his son, a note to the Rev. F. Prince will find him there.

Miss Clapperclaw says we are both a couple of old fools ; and that she knew when I set off last year to Rodwell Regis, after meeting the two young ladies at a party at General Champion's house in our street, that I was going on a goose's errand. I shall dine there on Christmas-day ; and so I wish a merry Christmas to all young and old boys.

EPILOGUE.

The play is done ; the curtain drops,
  Slow falling, to the prompter's bell :
A moment yet the actor stops,
  And looks around, to say farewell.
It is an irksome word and task ;
  And when he 's laughed and said his say,
He shows, as he removes the mask,
  A face that 's anything but gay.

One word, ere yet the evening ends,
  Let 's close it with a parting rhyme,
And pledge a hand to all young friends,
  As fits the merry Christmas time.
On life's wide scene you, too, have parts,
  That Fate ere long shall bid you play ;
Good-night ! with honest gentle hearts
  A kindly greeting go alway !

Good-night ! I 'd say the griefs, the joys,
  Just hinted in this mimic page,
The triumphs and defeats of boys,
  Are but repeated in our age.
I 'd say, your woes were not less keen,
  Your hopes more vain, than those of men ;
Your pangs or pleasures of fifteen,
  At forty-five played o'er again.

I 'd say, we suffer and we strive
  Not less nor more as men than boys;
With grizzled beards at forty-five,
  As erst at twelve, in corduroys.
And if, in time of sacred youth,
  We learned at home to love and pray,
Pray Heaven, that early love and truth
  May never wholly pass away.

And in the world, as in the school,
  I 'd say, how fate may change and shift;
The prize be sometimes with the fool,
  The race not always to the swift.
The strong may yield, the good may fall,
  The great man be a vulgar clown,
The knave be lifted over all,
  The kind cast pitilessly down.

Who knows the inscrutable design?
  Blessed be He who took and gave:
Why should your mother, Charles, not mine,
  Be weeping at her darling's grave? [1]
We bow to Heaven that will'd it so,
  That darkly rules the fate of all,
That sends the respite or the blow,
  That 's free to give or to recall.

This crowns his feast with wine and wit:
  Who brought him to that mirth and state?

[1] C. B., ob. Dec. 1843, æt. 42.

His betters, see, below him sit,
  Or hunger hopeless at the gate.
Who bade the mud from Dives' Wheel
  To spurn the rags of Lazarus ?
Come, brother, in that dust we 'll kneel,
  Confessing Heaven that ruled it thus.

So each shall mourn in life's advance,
  Dear hopes, dear friends, untimely killed ;
Shall grieve for many a forfeit chance,
  A longing passion unfulfilled.
Amen : whatever Fate be sent, —
  Pray God the heart may kindly glow,
Although the head with cares be bent,
  And whitened with the winter snow.

Come wealth or want, come good or ill,
  Let young and old accept their part,
And bow before the Awful Will,
  And bear it with an honest heart.
Who misses, or who wins the prize ?
  Go, lose or conquer as you can :
But if you fail, or if you rise,
  Be each, pray God, a gentleman,

A gentleman, or old or young :
  (Bear kindly with my humble lays,)
The sacred chorus first was sung
  Upon the first of Christmas days.

The shepherds heard it overhead —
   The joyful angels raised it then :
Glory to Heaven on high, it said,
   And peace on earth to gentle men.

My song, save this, is little worth ;
   I lay the weary pen aside,
And wish you health, and love, and mirth,
   As fits the solemn Christmas tide.
As fits the holy Christmas birth,
   Be this, good friends, our carol still —
Be peace on earth, be peace on earth,
   To men of gentle will.

THE BOOK OF SNOBS.

BY ONE OF THEMSELVES.

PREFATORY REMARKS.

[The necessity of a work on Snobs, demonstrated from History, and proved by felicitous illustrations : — I am the individual destined to write that work — My vocation is announced in terms of great eloquence — I show that the world has been gradually preparing itself for the WORK *and the* MAN *— Snobs are to be studied like other objects of Natural Science, and are a part of the Beautiful (with a large B). They pervade all classes — Affecting instance of Colonel Snobley.]*

WE have all read a statement (the authenticity of which I take leave to doubt entirely, for upon what calculations I should like to know is it founded ?) — we have all, I say, been favored by perusing a remark, that when the times and necessities of the world call for a Man, that individual is found. Thus at the French Revolution (which the reader will be pleased to have introduced so early),

when it was requisite to administer a corrective
dose to the nation, Robespierre was found ; a
most foul and nauseous dose indeed, and swallowed eagerly by the patient, greatly to the
latter's ultimate advantage ; thus, when it became necessary to kick John Bull out of
America, Mr. Washington stepped forward and
performed that job to satisfaction ; thus, when
the Earl of Aldborough was unwell, Professor
Holloway appeared with his pills, and cured
his lordship, as per advertisement, etc., etc.
Numberless instances might be adduced to show
that when a nation is in great want, the relief
is at hand ; just as in the Pantomime (that
microcosm) where when *Clown* wants anything
— a warming-pan, a pump-handle, a goose, or
a lady's tippet — a fellow comes sauntering out
from behind the side-scenes with the very article in question.

Again, when men commence an undertaking,
they always are prepared to show that the ab-
solute necessities of the world demanded its
completion. — Say it is a railroad : the directors
begin by stating that " A more intimate com-
munication between Bathershins and Derrynane
Beg is necessary for the advancement of civilization, and demanded by the multitudinous
acclamations of the great Irish people." Or

suppose it is a newspaper : the prospectus
states that " At a time when the Church is in
danger, threatened from without by savage
fanaticism and miscreant unbelief, and under-
mined from within by dangerous Jesuitism and
suicidal Schism, a Want has been universally
felt — a suffering people has looked abroad —
for an Ecclesiastical Champion and Guardian.
A body of Prelates and Gentlemen have therefore stepped forward in this our hour of danger,
and determined on establishing the *Beadle* newspaper," etc., etc.   One or other of these points
at least is incontrovertible : the public wants a
thing, therefore it is supplied with it ; or the
public is supplied with a thing ; therefore it
wants it.

I have long gone about with a conviction on
my mind that I had a work to do — a Work, if
you like, with a great W ; a Purpose to fulfill ;
a chasm to leap into, like Curtius, horse &
foot ; a Great Social Evil to Discover and to
Remedy.   That Conviction Has Pursued me
for Years.   It has Dogged me in the Busy
Street ; Seated Itself By me in The Lonely
Study ; Jogged my Elbow as it Lifted the
Wine-cup at The Festive Board ; pursued me
through the Maze of Rotten Row ; Followed
me in Far Lands.   On Brighton's Shingly

Beach, or Margate's Sand, the Voice Outpiped
the Roaring of the Sea ; it Nestles in my Night-
cap, and It Whispers " Wake, Slumberer, thy
Work Is Not Yet Done." Last Year, By
Moonlight, in the Colosseum, the Little Sedu-
lous Voice Came to me and Said, " Smith, or
Jones " (The Writer's Name is Neither Here
nor There), " Smith or Jones, my fine fellow,
this is all very well, but you ought to be at
home writing your great work on SNOBS."

When a man has this sort of vocation it is
all nonsense attempting to elude it. He must
speak out to the nations ; he must *unbusm* himself, as Jeames would say, or choke and die.
"Mark to yourself," I have often mentally exclaimed to your humble servant, " the gradual
way in which you have been prepared for, and
are now led by an irresistible necessity to enter
upon your great labor. First, the World was
made : then, as a matter of course, Snobs ; they
existed for years and years, and were no more
known than America. But presently — *ingens
patebat tellus* — the people became darkly aware
that there was such a race. Not above five-
and-twenty years since, a name, an expressive
monosyllable, arose to designate that race.
That name has spread over England like rail-
roads subsequently ; Snobs are known and

recognized throughout an Empire on which I
am given to understand the Sun never sets.
Punch appears at the ripe reason, to chronicle
their history : and the individual comes forth
to write that history in *Punch*." [1]

I have (and for this gift I congratulate myself with a Deep and Abiding thankfulness) an
eye for a Snob. If the Truthful is the Beautiful, it is Beautiful to study even the Snobbish ;
to track Snobs through history, as certain little
dogs in Hampshire hunt out truffles ; to sink
shafts in society and come upon rich veins of
Snob - ore. Snobbishness is like Death in a
quotation from Horace, which I hope you never
have heard, " beating with equal foot at poor
men's doors, and kicking at the gates of Emper-
ors." It is a great mistake to judge of Snobs
lightly, and think they exist among the lower
classes merely. An immense percentage of
Snobs, I believe, is to be found in every rank
of this mortal life. You must not judge hastily
or vulgarly of Snobs : to do so shows that you
are yourself a Snob. I myself have been taken
for one.

When I was taking the waters at Bagniggie
Wells, and living at the " Imperial Hotel "

---

[1] These papers were originally published in that popular
periodical.

there, there used to sit opposite me at breakfast, for a short time, a Snob so insufferable
that I felt I should never get any benefit of the
waters so long as he remained. His name was
Lieutenant-Colonel Snobley, of a certain dragoon
regiment. He wore japanned boots and moustaches ; he lisped, drawled, and left the " r's "
out of his words ; he was always flourishing
about and smoothing his lacquered whiskers
with a huge flaming bandanna, that filled the
room with an odor of musk so stifling that I
determined to do battle with that Snob, and
that either he or I should quit the Inn. I first
began harmless conversations with him ; fright-
ening him exceedingly, for he did not know
what to do when so attacked, and had never
the slightest notion that anybody would take
such a liberty with him as to speak *first :* then
I handed him the paper : then, as he would
take no notice of these advances, I used to look
him in the face steadily and — and use my fork
in the light of a toothpick. After two mornings
of this practice, he could bear it no longer, and
fairly quitted the place.

Should the Colonel see this, will he remember
the Gent who asked him if he thought Publi-
coaler was a fine writer, and drove him from
the hotel with a four-pronged fork ?

THE SNOB PLAYFULLY DEALT WITH.

THERE are relative and positive Snobs. I mean by positive, such persons as are Snobs everywhere, in all companies, from morning till night, from youth to the grave, being by Nature endowed with Snobbishness — and others who are Snobs only in certain circumstances and relations of life.

For instance : I once knew a man who committed before me an act as atrocious as that which I have indicated in the last chapter as performed by me for the purpose of disgusting Colonel Snobley ; viz., the using the fork in the guise of a toothpick. I once, I say, knew a man who, dining in my company at the " Europa Coffee-house " (opposite the Grand Opera, and, as everybody knows, the only decent place for dining at Naples), ate peas with the assistance of his knife. He was a person with whose society I was greatly pleased at first — indeed, we had met in the crater of Vesuvius, and were subsequently robbed and held to ransom by brigands in Calabria, which is nothing to the purpose — a man of great powers, excellent heart, and varied information ; but I had never before seen him with a dish of peas, and his conduct in regard to them caused me the deepest pain.

After having seen him thus publicly comport himself, but one course was open to me — to cut his acquaintance. I commissioned a mutual friend (the Honorable Poly Anthus) to break the matter to this gentleman as delicately as possible, and to say that painful circumstances — in nowise affecting Mr. Marrowfat's honor, or my esteem for him — had occurred, which obliged me to forego my intimacy with him ; and accordingly we met, and gave each other the cut direct that night at the Duchess of Monte Fiasco's ball.

Everybody at Naples remarked the separation of the Damon and Pythias — indeed, Marrowfat had saved my life more than once — but as an English gentleman, what was I to do ?

My dear friend was, in this instance, the Snob *relative*. It is not snobbish of persons of rank of any other nation to employ their knife in the manner alluded to. I have seen Monte Fiasco clean his trencher with his knife, and every Principe in company doing likewise. I have seen, at the hospitable board of H. I. H. the Grand Duchess Stephanie of Baden — (who, if these humble lines should come under her Imperial eyes, is besought to remember graciously the most devoted of her servants) — I have seen, I say, the Hereditary Princess of Potztausend-Donnerwetter (that serenely-beautiful woman) use her knife in lieu of a fork or spoon ; I have seen her almost swallow it, by Jove ! like Ramo Samee, the Indian juggler. And did I blench ? Did my estimation for the Princess diminish ? No, lovely Amalia ! One of the truest passions that ever was inspired by woman was raised in this bosom by that lady ! Beautiful one ! long, long may the knife carry food to those lips ! the reddest and loveliest in the world.

The cause of my quarrel with Marrowfat I never breathed to mortal soul for four years. We met in the halls of the aristocracy — our friends and relatives. We jostled each other in the dance or at the board ; but the estrangement continued, and seemed irrevocable, until the fourth of June, last year.

We met at Sir George Golloper's. We were placed, he on the right, your humble servant on the left, of the admirable Lady G. Peas formed part of the banquet — ducks and green peas. I trembled as I saw Marrowfat helped, and turned away sickening, lest I should behold the weapon darting down his horrid jaws.

What was my astonishment, what my delight, when I saw him use his fork like any other Christian! He did not administer the cold steel once. Old times rushed back upon me — the remembrance of old services — his rescuing me from the brigands — his gallant conduct in the affair with the Countess Dei Spinachi — his lending me the 1,700*l*. I almost burst into tears with joy — my voice trembled with emotion. "George, my boy!" I exclaimed, "George Marrowfat, my dear fellow! a glass of wine!"

Blushing — deeply moved — almost as tremulous as I was myself, George answered, "*Frank, shall it be Hock or Madeira?*" I could have hugged him to my heart but for the presence of the company. Little did Lady Golloper know what was the cause of the emotion which sent the duckling I was carving into her ladyship's pink satin lap. The most good-natured of women pardoned the error, and the butler removed the bird.

We have been the closest friends ever since, nor, of course, has George repeated his odious habit. He acquired it at a country school, where they cultivated peas and only used two-pronged forks, and it was only by living on the Continent, where the usage of the four-prong is general, that he lost the horrible custom.

In this point — and in this only — I confess myself a member of the Silver-Fork School ; and if this tale but induce one of my readers to pause, to examine in his own mind solemnly, and ask, "Do I or do I not eat peas with a knife ? " — to see the ruin which may fall upon himself by continuing the practice, or his family by beholding the example, these lines will not have been written in vain.　And now, whatever other authors may be, I flatter myself, it will be allowed that *I*, at least, am a moral man.

By the way, as some readers are dull of comprehension, I may as well say what the moral of this history is.　The moral is this — Society having ordained certain customs, men are bound to obey the law of society, and conform to its harmless orders.

If I should go to the British and Foreign Institute (and Heaven forbid I should go under any pretext or in any costume whatever) — if I should go to one of the tea-parties in a dressing-gown and slippers, and not in the usual attire of a gentleman, viz., pumps, a gold waistcoat, a crush hat, a sham frill, and a white choker — I should be insulting society, and *eating peas with my knife.*　Let the porters of the Institute hustle out the individual who shall so offend.

Such an offender is, as regards society, a. most emphatical and refractory Snob. It has its code and police as well as governments, and he must conform who would profit by the decrees set forth for their common comfort.

I am naturally averse to egotism, and hate self-laudation consumedly; but I can't help relating here a circumstance illustrative of the point in question, in which I must think I acted with considerable prudence.

Being at Constantinople a few years since — (on a delicate mission) — the Russians were playing a double game, between ourselves, and it became necessary on our part to employ an *extra negotiator* — Leckerbiss Pasha of Roumelia, then Chief Galeongee of the Porte, gave a diplomatic banquet at his summer palace at Bujukdere. I was on the left of the Galeongee, and the Russian agent, Count de Diddloff, on his dexter side. Diddloff is a dandy who would die of a rose in aromatic pain : he had tried to have me assassinated three times in the course of the negotiation ; but of course we were friends in public, and saluted each other in the most cordial and charming manner.

The Galeongee is — or was, alas ! for a bow-string has done for him — a stanch supporter of the old school of Turkish politics. We dined with our fingers, and had flaps of bread for plates ; the only innovation he admitted was the use of European liquors, in which he indulged with great gusto. He was an enormous eater. Amongst the dishes a very large one was placed before him of a lamb dressed in its wool, stuffed with prunes, garlic, asafœtida, capsicums, and other condiments, the most abominable mixture that ever mortal smelt or tasted. The Galeongee ate of this hugely ; and, pursuing the Eastern fashion, insisted on helping his friends right and left, and when he came to a particularly spicy morsel, would push it with his own hands into his guests' very mouths.

I never shall forget the look of poor Diddloff, when his Excellency, rolling up a large quantity of this into a ball and exclaiming, "Buk Buk" (it is very good), administered the horrible bolus to Diddloff. The Russian's eyes rolled dreadfully as he received it : he swallowed it with a grimace that I thought must precede a convulsion, and seizing a bottle next him, which he thought was Sauterne, but which turned out to be French brandy, he drank off nearly a pint before he knew his error. It finished him ; he was carried away from the dining-room almost dead, and laid out to cool in a summer-house on the Bosphorus.

When it came to my turn, I took down the condiment with a smile, said "Bismillah," licked my lips with easy gratification, and when the next dish was served, made up a ball myself so dexterously, and popped it down the old Galeongee's mouth with so much grace, that his heart was won. Russia was put out of court at once, *and the treaty of* Kabobanople *was signed*. As for Diddloff, all was over with *him:* he was recalled to St. Petersburg, and Sir Roderick Murchison saw him, under the No. 3967, working in the Ural mines.

The moral of this tale, I need not say, is, that there are many disagreeable things in society which you are bound to take down, and to do so with a smiling face.

ROUNDABOUT PAPERS.[1]

THORNS IN THE CUSHION.

IN the Essay with which this volume commences, the *Cornhill Magazine* was likened to a ship sailing forth on her voyage, and the captain uttered a very sincere prayer for her prosperity. The dangers of storm and rock, the vast outlay upon ship and cargo, and the certain risk of the venture, gave the chief officer a feeling of no small anxiety; for who could say from what quarter danger might arise, and how his owner's property might be imperiled? After a six months' voyage, we with very thankful hearts could acknowledge our good fortune: and, taking up the apologue in the Roundabout manner, we composed a triumphal procession in honor of the Magazine, and imagined the Imperator thereof riding in

---

[1] Published in the *Cornhill Magazine*, of which Thackeray was the first editor.

a sublime car to return thanks in the Temple
of Victory.   Cornhill is accustomed to grandeur
and greatness, and has witnessed, every 9th of
November, for I don't know how many centuries, a prodigious annual pageant, chariot,
progress, and flourish of trumpetry ; and being
so very near the Mansion House, I am sure the
reader will understand how the idea of pageant
and procession came naturally to my mind.
The imagination easily supplied a gold coach,
eight cream-colored horses of your true Pegasus
breed, huzzaing multitudes, running footmen,
and clanking knights in armor, a chaplain and
a sword-bearer with a muff on his head, scowling out of the coach-window, and a Lord Mayor
all crimson, fur, gold chain, and white ribbons,
solemnly occupying the place of state.   A playful fancy could have carried the matter farther,
could have depicted the feast in the Egyptian
Hall, the Ministers, Chief Justices, and right
reverend prelates taking their seats round
about his lordship, the turtle and other delicious
viands, and Mr. Toole behind the central
throne, bawling out to the assembled guests and
dignitaries : "My Lord So-and-So, my Lord
What-d'ye-call-'im, my Lord Etcætera, the
Lord Mayor pledges you all in a loving-cup."
Then the noble proceedings come to an end ;

Lord Simper proposes the ladies ; the company
rises from table, and adjourns to coffee and
muffins.   The carriages of the nobility and
guests roll back to the West.   The Egyptian
Hall, so bright just now, appears in a twilight
glimmer, in which waiters are seen ransacking
the dessert, and rescuing the spoons.   His lordship and the Lady Mayoress go into their private apartments.   The robes are doffed, the
collar and white ribbons are removed.   The
Mayor becomes a man, and is pretty surely in
a fluster about the speeches which he has just
uttered ; remembering too well now, wretched
creature, the principal points which he *did n't*
make when he rose to speak.   He goes to bed
to headache, to care, to repentance, and, I dare
say, to a dose of something which his body-
physician has prescribed for him.   And there
are ever so many men in the city who fancy
that man happy !

Now, suppose that all through that 9th of
November his lordship has had a racking rheumatism, or a toothache, let us say, during all
dinner-time — through which he has been
obliged to grin and mumble his poor old
speeches.   Is he enviable ?   Would you like to
change with his lordship ?   Suppose that
bumper which his golden footman brings him,

instead i'fackins of ypocras or canary, contains some abomination of senna? Away! Remove the golden goblet, insidious cup-bearer! You now begin to perceive the gloomy moral which I am about to draw.

Last month we sang the song of glorification, and rode in the chariot of triumph. It was all very well. It was right to huzza, and be thankful, and cry, Bravo, our side! and besides, you know there was the enjoyment of thinking how pleased Brown, and Jones, and Robinson (our dear friends) would be at this announcement of success. But now that the performance is over, my good sir, just step into my private room, and see that it is not all pleasure — this winning of successes. Cast your eye over those newspapers, over those letters. See what the critics say of your harmless jokes, neat little trim sentences, and pet waggeries! Why, you are no better than an idiot; you are driveling; your powers have left you; this always overrated writer is rapidly sinking to, etc.

This is not pleasant; but neither is this the point. It may be the critic is right, and the author wrong. It may be that the archbishop's sermon is not so fine as some of those discourses twenty years ago which used to delight the faithful in Granada. Or it may be (pleasing

thought !) that the critic is a dullard, and does
not understand what he is writing about. Everybody who has been to an exhibition has heard
visitors discoursing about the pictures before
their faces. One says, "This is very well ; "
another says, "This is stuff and rubbish ; "
another cries, "Bravo ! this is a masterpiece : "
and each has a right to his opinion. For example, one of the pictures I admired most at
the Royal Academy is by a gentleman on whom
I never, to my knowledge, set eyes. This picture is No. 346, "Moses," by Mr. S. Solomon.
I thought it had a great intention, I thought it
finely drawn and composed. It nobly represented to my mind the dark children of the
Egyptian bondage, and suggested the touching
story. My newspaper says : " Two ludicrously
ugly women, looking at a dingy baby, do not
form a pleasing object ; " and so good-by, Mr.
Solomon. Are not most of our babies served
so in life ? and does n't Mr. Robinson consider
Mr. Brown's cherub an ugly, squalling little
brat ? So cheer up, Mr. S. S. It may be the
critic who discoursed on your baby is a bad
judge of babies. When Pharaoh's kind daughter found the child, and cherished and loved
it, and took it home, and found a nurse for
it, too, I dare say there were grim, brick-

dust colored chamberlains, or some of the tough, old, meagre, yellow princesses at court, who never had children themselves, who cried out, "Faugh! the horrid little squalling wretch!" and knew he would never come to good; and said, "Did n't I tell you so?" when he assaulted the Egyptian.

Never mind, then, Mr. S. Solomon, I say, because a critic pooh-poohs your work of art — your Moses — your child — your foundling. Why, did not a wiseacre in *Blackwood's Magazine* lately fall foul of "Tom Jones"? O hypercritic! So, to be sure, did good old Mr. Richardson, who could write novels himself — but you, and I, and Mr. Gibbon, my dear sir, agree in giving our respect, and wonder, and admiration, to the brave old master.

In these last words I am supposing the respected reader to be endowed with a sense of humor, which he may or may not possess; indeed, don't we know many an honest man who can no more comprehend a joke than he can turn a tune? But I take for granted, my dear sir, that you are brimming over with fun — you may n't make jokes, but you could if you would — you know you could: and in your quiet way you enjoy them extremely. Now many people neither make them, nor understand them when

made, nor like them when understood, and are
suspicious, testy, and angry with jokers. Have
you ever watched an elderly male or female —
an elderly "party," so to speak, who begins to
find out that some young wag of the company
is "chaffing" him? Have you ever tried the
sarcastic or Socratic method with a child?
Little simple he or she, in the innocence of the
simple heart, plays some silly freak, or makes
some absurd remark, which you turn to ridicule.
The little creature dimly perceives that you are
making fun of him, writhes, blushes, grows
uneasy, bursts into tears, — upon my word it is
not fair to try the weapon of ridicule upon that
innocent young victim. The awful objurgatory
practice he is accustomed to. Point out his
fault, and lay bare the dire consequences thereof : expose it roundly, and give him a proper,
solemn, moral whipping — but do not attempt
to *castigare ridendo.* Do not laugh at him
writhing, and cause all the other boys in the
school to laugh. Remember your own young
days at school, my friend — the tingling cheeks,
burning ears, bursting heart, and passion of
desperate tears, with which you looked up, after
having performed some blunder, whilst the
doctor held you to public scorn before the class,
and cracked his great clumsy jokes upon you —

helpless, and a prisoner! Better the block itself, and the lictors, with their fasces of birch-twigs, than the maddening torture of those jokes!

Now with respect to jokes — and the present company of course excepted — many people, perhaps most people, are as infants. They have little sense of humor. They don't like jokes. Raillery in writing annoys and offends them. The coarseness apart, I think I have met very, very few women who liked the banter of Swift and Fielding. Their simple, tender natures revolt at laughter. Is the satyr always a wicked brute at heart, and are they rightly shocked at his grin, his leer, his horns, hoofs, and ears? *Fi donc, le vilain monstre,* with his shrieks, and his capering crooked legs! Let him go and get a pair of well-wadded black silk stockings, and pull them over those horrid shanks; put a large gown and bands over beard and hide; and pour a dozen of lavender-water into his lawn handkerchief, and cry, and never make a joke again. It shall all be highly-dis-tilled poesy, and perfumed sentiment, and gush-ing eloquence; and the foot *sha'n't* peep out, and a plague take it. Cover it up with the surplice. Out with your cambric, dear ladies, and let us all whimper together.

Now, then, hand on heart, we declare that it is not the fire of adverse critics which afflicts or frightens the editorial bosom. They may be right ; they may be rogues who have a personal spite ; they may be dullards who kick and bray as their nature is to do, and prefer thistles to pineapples ; they may be conscientious, acute, deeply learned, delightful judges, who see your joke in a moment, and the profound wisdom lying underneath. Wise or dull, laudatory or otherwise, we put their opinions aside. If they applaud, we are pleased : if they shake their quick pens, and fly off with a hiss, we resign their favors and put on all the fortitude we can muster. I would rather have the lowest man's good word than his bad one, to be sure ; but as for coaxing a compliment, or wheedling him into good-humor, or stopping his angry mouth with a good dinner, or accepting his contributions for a certain Magazine, for fear of his barking or snapping elsewhere — *allons donc!* These shall not be our acts. Bow-wow, Cerberus ! Here shall be no sop for thee, unless — unless Cerberus is an uncommonly good dog, when we shall bear no malice because he flew at us from a neighbor's gate.

What, then, is the main grief you spoke of

as annoying you — the toothache in the Lord
Mayor's jaw, the thorn in the cushion of the
editorial chair ? It is there. Ah ! it stings me
now as I write. It comes with almost every
morning's post. At night I come home and
take my letters up to bed (not daring to open
them), and in the morning I find one, two,
three thorns on my pillow. Three I extracted
yesterday ; two I found this morning. They
don't sting quite so sharply as they did ; but a
skin is a skin, and they bite, after all, most
wickedly. It is all very fine to advertise on
the Magazine, "Contributions are only to be
sent to Messrs. Smith, Elder and Co., and not
to the Editor's private residence." My dear
sir, how little you know man or woman kind,
if you fancy they will take that sort of warn-
ing ! How am I to know (though, to be sure,
I begin to know now), as I take the letters off
the tray, which of those envelopes contains a
real *bona fide* letter, and which a thorn ? One
of the best invitations this year I mistook for a
thorn-letter, and kept it without opening. This
is what I call a thorn-letter : —

"CAMBERWELL. June 4.

"SIR, — May I hope, may I entreat, that you will
favor me by perusing the inclosed lines, and that

they may be found worthy of insertion in the *Cornhill Magazine?* We have known better days, sir. I have a sick and widowed mother to maintain, and little brothers and sisters who look to me. I do my utmost as governess to support them. I toil at night when they are at rest, and my own hand and brain are alike tired. If I could add but *a little* to our means by my pen, many of my poor invalid's wants might be supplied, and I could procure for her comforts to which she is now a stranger. Heaven knows it is not for want of *will* or for want of *energy* on my part, that she is now in ill-health, and our little household almost without bread. Do — do cast a kind glance over my poem, and if you can help us, the widow, the orphans will bless you! I remain, sir, in anxious expectancy,

" Your faithful servant,   S. S. S."

And inclosed is a little poem or two, and an envelope with its penny stamp — heaven help us ! — and the writer's name and address.

Now you see what I mean by a thorn. Here is the case put with true female logic. "I am poor; I am good; I am ill; I work hard; I have a sick mother and hungry brothers and sisters dependent on me. You can help us if you will." And then I look at the paper, with the thousandth part of a faint hope that it may be suitable, and I find it won't do : and I knew it wouldn't do : and why is this poor lady to appeal to my pity and bring her poor little ones

kneeling to my bedside, and calling for bread
which I can give them if I choose? No day
passes but that argument *ad misericordiam* is
used. Day and night that sad voice is crying
out for help. Thrice it appealed to me yesterday. Twice this morning it cried to me : and
I have no doubt when I go to get my hat, I
shall find it with its piteous face and its pale
family about it, waiting for me in the hall.
One of the immense advantages which women
have over our sex is, that they actually like to
read these letters. Like letters? O mercy on
us ! Before I was an editor I did not like the
postman much : — but now !

A very common way with these petitioners is
to begin with a fine flummery about the merits
and eminent genius of the person whom they
are addressing. But this artifice, I state publicly, is of no avail. When I see *that* kind of
herb, I know the snake within it, and fling it
away before it has time to sting. Away, rep-
tile, to the waste-paper basket, and thence to
the flames !

But of these disappointed people, some take
their disappointment and meekly bear it. Some
hate and hold you their enemy because you
could not be their friend. Some, furious and
envious, say : " Who is this man who refuses

what I offer, and how dares he, the conceited coxcomb, to deny my merit ? "

Sometimes my letters contain not mere thorns, but bludgeons. Here are two choice slips from that noble Irish oak, which has more than once supplied alpeens for this meek and un-offending skull : —

"THEATRE ROYAL, DONNYBROOK.

" SIR, — I have just finished reading the first por-tion of your Tale, *Lovel the Widower*, and am much surprised at the unwarrantable strictures you pass therein on the *corps de ballet*.

" I have been for more than ten years connected with the theatrical profession, and I beg to assure you that the majority of the *corps de ballet* are vir-tuous, well-conducted girls, and, consequently, that snug cottages are not taken for them in the Regent's Park.

" I also have to inform you that theatrical man-agers are in the habit of speaking good English, possibly better English than authors.

" You either know nothing of the subject in ques-tion, or you assert a willful falsehood.

" I am happy to say that the characters of the *corps de ballet*, as also those of actors and actresses, are superior to the snarling of dyspeptic libelers, or the spiteful attacks and *brutum fulmen* of ephemeral authors.   I am, sir, your obedient servant,

"A. B. C."

The Editor of the *Cornhill Magazine*.

"THEATRE ROYAL, DONNYBROOK.

"SIR, — I have just read in the *Cornhill Magazine* for January, the first portion of a Tale written by you, and entitled *Lovel the Widower*.

" In the production in question you employ all your malicious spite (and you have great capabilities that way) in trying to degrade the character of the *corps de ballet*. When you imply that the majority of ballet-girls have villas taken for them in the Regent's Park, *I say you tell a deliberate falsehood*.

" Having been brought up to the stage from infancy, and though now an actress, having been seven years principal dancer at the opera, I am competent to speak on the subject. I am only surprised that so vile a libeler as yourself should be allowed to preside at the Dramatic Fund dinner on the 22d instant. I think it would be much better if you were to reform your own life, instead of telling lies of those who are immeasurably your superiors.

" Yours in supreme disgust, A. D."

The signatures of the respected writers are altered, and for the site of their Theatre Royal an adjacent place is named, which (as I may have been falsely informed) used to be famous for quarrels, thumps, and broken heads. But, I say, is this an easy chair to sit on, when you are liable to have a pair of such shillelahs flung at it ? And, prithee, what was all the quarrel about ? In the little history of "Lovel the Widower " I described, and brought to condign

punishment, a certain wretch of a ballet-dancer,
who lived splendidly for a while on ill-gotten
gains, had an accident, and lost her beauty, and
died poor, deserted, ugly, and every way odious.
On the same page, other little ballet-dancers
are described, wearing homely clothing, doing
their duty, and carrying their humble savings
to the family at home. But nothing will content my dear correspondents but to have me
declare that the majority of ballet-dancers have
villas in the Regent's Park, and to convict me
of "deliberate falsehood." Suppose, for instance, I had chosen to introduce a red-haired
washerwoman into a story? I might get an
expostulatory letter saying, "Sir, in stating
that the majority of washerwomen are red-
haired, you are a liar! and you had best not
speak of ladies who are immeasurably your
superiors." Or suppose I had ventured to
describe an illiterate haberdasher? One of
the craft might write to me, "Sir, in describing
haberdashers as illiterate, you utter a willful
falsehood. Haberdashers use much better
English than authors." It is a mistake, to be
sure. I have never said what my correspondents say I say. There is the text under their
noses, but what if they choose to read it their
own way? "Hurroo, lads! Here's for a

fight. There's a bald head peeping out of the hut. There's a bald head! It must be Tim Malone's." And whack! come down both the bludgeons at once.

Ah me! we wound where we never intended to strike; we create anger where we never meant harm; and these thoughts are the thorns in our Cushion. Out of mere malignity, I suppose, there is no man who would like to make enemies. But here, in this editorial business, you can't do otherwise: and a queer, sad, strange, bitter thought it is, that must cross the mind of many a public man: "Do what I will, be innocent or spiteful, be generous or cruel, there are A and B, and C and D, who will hate me to the end of the chapter — to the chapter's end — to the Finis of the page — when hate, and envy, and fortune, and disappointment shall be over."

ON SCREENS IN DINING-ROOMS.

A GRANDSON of the late Rev. Dr. Primrose (of Wakefield, vicar) wrote me a little note from his country living this morning, and the kind fellow had the precaution to write "No thorn" upon the envelope, so that, ere I broke the seal, my mind might be relieved of any anxiety lest the letter should contain one of those lurking stabs which are so painful to the present gentle writer. Your epigraph, my dear P., shows your kind and artless nature ; but don't you see it is of no use ? People who are bent upon assassinating you in the manner mentioned will write " No thorn " upon their envelopes too : and you open the case, and presently out flies a poisoned stiletto, which springs into a man's bosom, and makes the wretch howl with anguish. When the bailiffs are after a man, they adopt all sorts of disguises, pop out on him from all conceivable corners, and tap his miserable shoulders. His wife is taken ill ; his sweetheart, who remarked his brilliant, too brilliant appearance at the Hyde Park review, will meet him at Cremorne or where you will. The old friend who has owed him that money these five years will meet him at so-and-so and pay. By one bait or other the victim is hooked, netted, landed, and down goes the basket-lid. It is not your wife, your sweetheart, your friend who is going to pay you. It is Mr. Nab, the bailiff. *You* know — you are caught. You are off in a cab to Chancery Lane.

You know, I say ? *Why* should you know ?

I make no manner of doubt you never were taken by a baliff in your life. I never was. I have been in two or three debtors' prisons, but not on my own account. Goodness be praised! I mean you can't escape your lot, and Nab only stands here metaphorically as the watchful, certain, and untiring officer of Mr. Sheriff Fate. Why, my dear Primrose, this morning along with your letter comes another, bearing the well-known superscription of another old friend, which I open without the least suspicion, and what do I find? A few lines from my friend Johnson, it is true, but they are written on a page covered with feminine handwriting. "Dear Mr. Johnson," says the writer, "I have just been perusing with delight a most charming tale by the Archbishop of Cambray. It is called ' Telemachus ;' and I think it would be admirably suited to the *Cornhill Magazine.* As you know the editor, will you have the great kindness, dear Mr. Johnson, to communicate with him *personally* (as that is much better than writing in a roundabout way to the Publishers, and waiting goodness knows how long for an answer), and state my readiness to translate this excellent and instructive story. I do not wish to breathe *a word* against ' Lovel Parsonage,' ' Framley the Widower,' or any of the novels which have appeared in the *Cornhill Magazine*, but I *am sure* 'Telemachus' is as good as new to English readers, and in point of interest and morality *far*," etc., etc., etc.

There it is. I am stabbed through Johnson. He has lent himself to this attack on me. He is weak about women. Other strong men are. He submits to the common lot, poor fellow. In my reply I do not use a word of unkindness. I write him back gently, that I fear "Telemachus" won't suit us. He can send the letter on to his fair correspondent. But however soft the answer, I question whether the wrath will be turned away. Will there not be a coolness between him and the lady? and is it not possible that henceforth her fine eyes will look with darkling glances upon the pretty orange color of our magazine?

Certain writers, they say, have a bad opinion of women. Now I am very whimsical in supposing that this disappointed candidate will be hurt at her rejection, and angry or cast down according to her nature? "Angry, indeed!" says Juno, gathering up her purple robes and royal raiment. "Sorry, indeed!" cries Minerva, lacing on her corselet again, and scowling under her helmet. (I imagine the well-known Apple case has just been argued and decided.) Hurt,

forsooth! Do you suppose *we* care for the
opinion of that hobnailed lout of a Paris? Do
you suppose that I, the Goddess of Wisdom,
can't make allowances for mortal ignorance,
and am so base as to bear malice against a poor
creature who knows no better? You little
know the goddess nature when you dare to in-
sinuate that our divine minds are actuated by
motives so base. A love of justice influences
us. We are above mean revenge. We are too
magnanimous to be angry at the award of such
a judge in favor of such a creature." And
rustling out their skirts, the ladies walk away
together. This is all very well. You are
bound to believe them. They are actuated by
no hostility : not they. They bear no malice —
of course not. But when the Trojan war occurs
presently, which side will they take? Many
brave souls will be sent to Hades. Hector will
perish. Poor old Priam's bald numskull will
be cracked, and Troy town will burn, because
Paris prefers golden-haired Venus to ox-eyed
Juno and gray-eyed Minerva.

The last Essay of this Roundabout Series,
describing the griefs and miseries of the editorial chair, was written, as the kind reader
will acknowledge, in a mild and gentle, not in
a warlike or satirical spirit. I showed how

cudgels were applied ; but surely the meek
object of persecution hit no blows in return.
The beating did not hurt much, and the person
assaulted could afford to keep his good-humor ;
indeed, I admired that brave though illogical
little actress, of the T. R. D-bl-n, for her fiery
vindication of her profession's honor. I assure
her I had no intention to tell l — s — well, let
us say monosyllables — about my superiors :
and I wish her nothing but well, and when
Macmahon (or shall it be Mulligan ?) *Roi
d'Irlande* ascends his throne, I hope she may
be appointed professor of English to the princesses of the royal house. *Nuper* — in former
days — I too have militated ; sometimes, as I
now think, unjustly ; but always, I vow, without personal rancor. Which of us has not idle
words to recall, flippant jokes to regret ? Have
you never committed an imprudence ? Have
you never had a dispute, and found out that
you were wrong ? So much the worse for you.
Woe be to the man *qui croit toujours avoir raison.*
His anger is not a brief madness, but a perma-
nent mania. His rage is not a fever-fit, but a
black poison inflaming him, distorting his judgment, disturbing his rest, embittering his cup,
gnawing at his pleasures, causing him more
cruel suffering than ever he can inflict on his

enemy. *O la belle morale!* As I write it, I
think about one or two little affairs of my own.
There is old Dr. Squaretoso (he certainly was
very rude to me, and that 's the fact) ; there is
Madame Pomposa (and certainly her ladyship's
behavior was about as cool as cool could be).
Never mind, old Squaretoso : never mind,
Madame Pomposa ! Here is a hand. Let us
be friends as we once were, and have no more
of this rancor.

I had hardly sent that last Roundabout Paper
to the printer (which, I submit, was written in
a placable and not unchristian frame of mind),
when Saturday came, and with it, of course, my
Saturday Review. I remember at New York
coming down to breakfast at the hotel one
morning, after a criticism had appeared in the
New York Herald, in which an Irish writer had
given me a dressing for a certain lecture on
Swift. Ah ! my dear little enemy of the T. R.
D., what were the cudgels in *your* little *billet-
doux* compared to those noble New York
shillelahs ? All through the Union, the literary
sons of Erin have marched *alpeen*-stock in
hand, and in every city of the States they call
each other and everybody else the finest names.
Having come to breakfast, then, in the public
room, I sit down, and see — that the nine peo-

ple opposite have all got *New York Heralds* in their hands. One dear little lady, whom I knew, and who sat opposite, gave a pretty blush, and popped her paper under the tablecloth. I told her I had had my whipping already in my own private room, and begged her to continue her reading. I may have undergone agonies, you see, but every man who has been bred at an English public school comes away from a private interview with Dr. Birch with a calm, even a smiling face. And this is not impossible, when you are prepared. You screw your courage up — you go through the business. You come back and take your seat on the form, showing not the least symptom of uneasiness or of previous unpleasantries. But to be caught suddenly up, and whipped in the bosom of your family — to sit down to breakfast, and cast your innocent eye on a paper, and find, before you are aware, that the *Saturday Monitor* or *Black Monday Instructor* has hoisted you and is laying on — that is indeed a trial. Or perhaps the family has looked at the dreadful paper beforehand, and weakly tries to hide it. "Where is the *Instructor* or the *Monitor?*" say you. "Where is that paper?" says mamma to one of the young ladies. Lucy has n't it. Fanny has n't seen it. Emily thinks that the governess has it. At last, out it is brought, that awful paper ! Papa is amazingly tickled with the article on Thomson ; thinks that show up of Johnson is very lively ; and now — Heaven be good to us ! — he has come to the critique on himself : — " Of all rubbish which we have had from Mr. Tomkins, we do protest and vow that this last cartload is " etc. Ah, poor Tomkins ! — but most of all, ah ! poor Mrs. Tomkins, and poor Emily, and Fanny, and Lucy, who have to sit by and see *paterfamilias* put to the torture !

Now, on this eventful Saturday, I did not cry, because it was not so much the Editor as the Publisher of the *Cornhill Magazine* who was brought out for a dressing ; and it is wonderful how gallantly one bears the misfortunes of one's friends. That a writer should be taken to task about his books, is fair, and he must abide the praise or the censure. But that a publisher should be criticised for his dinners, and for the conversation which did *not* take place there, — is this tolerable press practice, legitimate joking, or honorable warfare ? I have not the honor to know my next-door neighbor, but I make no doubt that he receives his friends at dinner ; I see his wife and children pass constantly ; I even know the carriages of some of the people

who call upon him, and could tell their names.
Now, suppose his servants were to tell mine
what the doings are next door, who comes to
dinner, what is eaten and said, and I were to
publish an account of these transactions in a
newspaper, I could assuredly get money for the
report; but ought I to write it, and what would
you think of me for doing so?

And suppose, Mr. Saturday Reviewer — you
censor morum, you who pique yourself (and
justly and honorably in the main) upon your
character of gentleman, as well as of writer,
suppose, not that you yourself invent and indite
absurd twaddle about gentlemen's private meetings and transactions, but pick this wretched
garbage out of a New York street, and hold it
up for your reader's amusement — don't you
think, my friend, that you might have been
better employed?   Here, in my *Saturday Re-*
view, and in an American paper subsequently
sent to me, I light, astonished, on an account of
the dinners of my friend and publisher, which
are described as "tremendously heavy," of the
conversation (which does not take place), and
of the guests assembled at the table.   I am informed that the proprietor of the *Cornhill,* and
the host on these occasions, is "a very good
man, but totally unread;" and that on my

asking him whether Dr. Johnson was dining behind the screen, he said, "God bless my soul, my dear sir, there's no person by the name of Johnson here, nor any one behind the screen," and that a roar of laughter cut him short. I am informed by the same New York correspondent that I have touched up a contributor's article ; that I once said to a literary gentleman, who was proudly pointing to an anonymous article as his writing, " Ah ! I thought I recognized *your hoof* in it." I am told by the same authority that the *Cornhill Magazine* "shows symptoms of being on the wane," and having sold nearly a hundred thousand copies, he (the correspondent) "should think forty thousand was now about the mark." Then the graceful writer passes on to the dinners, at which it appears the Editor of the Magazine "is the great gun, and comes out with all the geniality in his power."

Now suppose this charming intelligence is untrue ? Suppose the publisher (to recall the noble words of my friend the Dublin actor of last month) is a gentleman to the full as well informed as those whom he invites to his table ? Suppose he never made the remark, beginning — "God bless my soul, my dear sir," etc., nor anything resembling it ? Suppose nobody roared with laughing? Suppose the Editor of the *Cornhill Magazine* never "touched up" one single line of the contribution which bears "marks of his hand"? Suppose he never said to any literary gentleman, "I recognize *your hoof*" in any periodical whatever? Suppose the 40,000 subscribers, which the writer to New York "considered to be about the mark," should be between 90,000 and 100,000 (and as he will have figures, there they are)? Suppose this back-door gossip should be utterly blundering and untrue, would any one wonder? Ah! if we had only enjoyed the happiness to number this writer among the contributors to our Magazine, what a cheerfulness and easy confidence his presence would impart to our meetings! He would find that "poor Mr. Smith" had heard that recondite anecdote of Dr. Johnson behind the screen; and as for "the great gun of those banquets," with what geniality should not I "come out" if I had an amiable companion close by me dotting down my conversation for the *New York Times!*

Attack our books, Mr. Correspondent, and welcome. They are fair subjects for just censure or praise. But woe be to you, if you allow private rancors or animosities to influence you in the discharge of your public duty. In the little court where you are paid to sit as judge, as critic, you owe it to your employers, to your conscience, to the honor of your calling, to deliver just sentences ; and you shall have to answer to Heaven for your dealings, as surely as my Lord Chief Justice on the Bench. The dignity of letters, the honor of the literary calling, the slights put by haughty and unthinking people upon literary men, — don't we hear outcries upon these subjects raised daily? As dear Sam Johnson sits behind the screen, too proud to show his threadbare coat and patches among the more prosperous brethren of his trade, there is no want of dignity in *him*, in that homely image of labor ill-rewarded, genius as yet unrecognized, independence sturdy and uncomplaining. But Mr. Nameless, behind the publisher's screen uninvited, peering at the company and the meal, catching up scraps of the jokes, and noting down the guests' behavior and conversation, — what a figure his is ! *Allons*, Mr. Nameless ! Put up your notebook ; walk out of the hall ; and leave gentlemen alone who would be private, and wish you no harm.

TUNBRIDGE TOYS.

I wonder whether those little silver pencil-cases with a movable almanac at the butt-end are still favorite implements with boys, and whether peddlers still hawk them about the country? Are there peddlers and hawkers still, or are rustics and children grown too sharp to deal with them? Those pencil-cases, as far as my memory serves me, were not of much use. The screw, upon which the movable almanac turned, was constantly getting loose. The 1 of the table would work from its moorings, under Tuesday or Wednesday, as the case might be, and you would find, on examination, that Th. or W. was the $23\frac{1}{2}$ of the month (which was absurd on the face of the thing), and in a word your cherished pencil-case an utterly unreliable time-keeper. Nor was this a matter of wonder. Consider the position of a pencil-case in a boy's pocket. You had hard-bake in it; marbles, kept in your purse when the money was all gone; your mother's purse knitted so fondly and supplied with a little bit of gold, long since — prodigal little son ! — scattered amongst the swine — I mean amongst brandy-balls, open tarts, three-cornered puffs,

and similar abominations. You had a top and
string ; a knife ; a piece of cobbler's wax ; two
or three bullets ; a *Little Warbler ;* and I, for
my part, remember, for a considerable period,
a brass-barreled pocket-pistol (which would
fire beautifully, for with it I shot off a button
from Butt Major's jacket) ; — with all these
things, and ever so many more, clinking and
rattling in your pockets, and your hands, of
course, keeping them in perpetual movement,
how could you expect your movable almanac
not to be twisted out of its place now and again
— your pencil-case to be bent — your liquorice-
water not to leak out of your bottle over the
cobbler's wax, your bull's-eyes not to ram up
the lock and barrel of your pistol, and so forth ?

In the month of June, thirty-seven years ago,
I bought one of those pencil-cases from a boy
whom I shall call Hawker, and who was in my
form. Is he dead ? Is he a millionnaire ? Is
he a bankrupt now ? He was an immense
screw at school, and I believe to this day that
the value of the thing for which I owed and
eventually paid three - and - sixpence, was in
reality not one-and-nine.

I certainly enjoyed the case at first a good
deal, and amused myself with twiddling round
the movable Calendar. But this pleasure wore

off. The jewel, as I said, was not paid for, and
Hawker, a large and violent boy, was exceedingly unpleasant as a creditor. His constant
remark was, "When are you going to pay me
that three-and-sixpence? What sneaks your
relations must be! They come to see you.
You go out to them on Saturdays and Sundays,
and they never give you anything! Don't
tell *me*, you little humbug!" and so forth. The
truth is that my relations were respectable;
but my parents were making a tour in Scot-
land; and my friends in London, whom I used
to go and see, were most kind to me, certainly,
but somehow never tipped me. That term, of
May to August, 1823, passed in agonies then,
in consequence of my debt to Hawker. What
was the pleasure of a calendar pencil-case in
comparison with the doubt and torture of mind
occasioned by the sense of the debt, and the
constant reproach of that fellow's scowling
eyes and gloomy, coarse reminders? How was
I to pay off such a debt out of sixpence a week?
ludicrous! Why did not some one come to see
me, and tip me? Ah, my dear sir, if you have
any little friends at school, go and see them,
and do the natural thing by them. You won't
miss the sovereign. You don't know what a
blessing it will be to them. Don't fancy they

are too old — try 'em. And they will remember you, and bless you in future days; and their gratitude shall accompany your dreary after-life; and they shall meet you kindly when thanks for kindness are scant. O mercy! shall I ever forget that sovereign you gave me, Captain Bob? or the agonies of being in debt to Hawker? In that very term, a relation of mine was going to India. I actually was fetched from school in order to take leave of him. I am afraid I told Hawker of this circumstance. I own I speculated upon my friend's giving me a pound. A pound? Pooh! A relation going to India, and deeply affected at parting from his darling kinsman, might give five pounds to the dear fellow! . . . There was Hawker when I came back — of course there he was. As he looked in my scared face, his turned livid with rage. He muttered curses, terrible from the lips of so young a boy. My relation, about to cross the ocean to fill a lucrative appointment, asked me with much interest about my progress at school, heard me construe a passage of Eutropius, the pleasing Latin work on which I was then engaged; gave me a God bless you, and sent me back to school; upon my word of honor, without so much as a half-crown! It is all very well, my dear sir, to say that boys contract habits of expecting tips from their parents' friends, that they became avaricious, and so forth. Avaricious! fudge! Boys contract habits of tart and toffee-eating, which they do not carry into after life. On the contrary, I wish I *did* like 'em. What raptures of pleasure one could have now for five shillings, if one could but pick it off the pastry-cook's tray! No. If you have any little friends at school, out with your half-crowns, my friend, and impart to those little ones the little fleeting joys of their age.

Well, then. At the beginning of August, 1823, Bartlemy-tide holidays came, and I was to go to my parents, who were at Tunbridge Wells. My place in the coach was taken by my tutor's servants — " Bolt-in-Tun," Fleet Street, seven o'clock in the morning, was the word. My tutor, the Rev. Edward P——, to whom I hereby present my best compliments, had a parting interview with me : gave me my little account for my governor : the remaining part of the coach-hire ; five shillings for my own expenses ; and some five and twenty shillings on an old account which had been over-paid, and was to be restored to my family.

Away I ran and paid Hawker his three-and-

six. Ouf! what a weight it was off my mind!
(He was a Norfolk boy, and used to go home
from Mrs. Nelson's "Bell Inn," Aldgate — but
that is not to the point). The next morning,
of course, we were an hour before the time. I
and another boy shared a hackney-coach ; two-
and-six : porter for putting luggage on coach,
threepence. I had no more money of my own
left. Rasherwell, my companion, went into
the "Bolt-in-Tun" coffee-room, and had a good
breakfast. I could n't ; because, though I had
five-and-twenty shillings of my parents' money,
I had none of my own, you see.

I certainly intended to go without breakfast,
and still remember how strongly I had that
resolution in my mind. But there was that
hour to wait. A beautiful August morning —
I am very hungry. There is Rasherwell "tuck-
ing" away in the coffee-room. I pace the
street, as sadly almost as if I had been coming
to school, not going thence. I turn into a court
by mere chance — I vow it was by mere chance
— and there I see a coffee-shop with a placard
in the window. *Coffee, Twopence. Round of
buttered toast, Twopence.* And here am I, hungry,
penniless, with five-and-twenty shillings of my
parents' money in my pocket.

What would you have done? You see I

had had my money, and spent it in that pencil-case affair. The five-and-twenty shillings were a trust — by me to be handed over.

But then would my parents wish their only child to be actually without breakfast? Having this money, and being so hungry, so *very* hungry, might n't I take ever so little? Might n't I at home eat as much as I chose?

Well, I went into the coffee-shop, and spent fourpence. I remember the taste of the coffee and toast to this day — a peculiar, muddy, not-sweet-enough, most fragrant coffee — a rich, rancid, yet not-buttered-enough, delicious toast. The waiter had nothing. At any rate, four-pence I know was the sum I spent. And the hunger appeased, I got on the coach a guilty being.

At the last stage, — what is its name? I have forgotten in seven-and-thirty years, — there is an inn with a little green and trees before it; and by the trees there is an open carriage. It is our carriage. Yes, there are Prince and Blucher, the horses; and my parents in the carriage. Oh! how I had been counting the days until this one came! Oh! how happy had I been to see them yesterday! But there was that fourpence. All the journey down the toast had choked me, and the coffee poisoned me.

I was in such a state of remorse about the fourpence, that I forgot the maternal joy and caresses, the tender paternal voice. I pull out the twenty-four shillings and eightpence with a trembling hand.

"Here's your money," I gasp out, "which Mr. P——owes you, all but fourpence. I owed three-and-sixpence to Hawker out of my money for a pencil-case, and I had none left, and I took fourpence of yours, and had some coffee at a shop."

I suppose I must have been choking whilst uttering this confession.

"My dear boy," says the governor, "why did n't you go and breakfast at the hotel?"

"He must be starved," says my mother.

I had confessed; I had been a prodigal; I had been taken back to my parents' arms again. It was not a very great crime as yet, or a very long career of prodigality; but don't we know that a boy who takes a pin which is not his own, will take a thousand pounds when occasion serves, bring his parents' gray heads with sorrow to the grave, and carry his own to the gallows? Witness the career of Dick Idle, upon whom · our friend Mr. Sala has been discoursing. Dick only began by playing pitch-and-toss on a tombstone : playing fair, for what we know :

and even for that sin he was promptly caned
by the beadle. The bamboo was ineffectual to
cane that reprobate's bad courses out of him.
From pitch-and-toss he proceeded to man-
slaughter if necessary : to highway robbery ; to
Tyburn and the rope there. Ah ! Heaven be
thanked, my parents' heads are still above the
grass, and mine still out of the noose.

As I look up from my desk, I see Tunbridge
Wells Common and the rocks, the strange
familiar place which I remember forty years
ago. Boys saunter over the green with stumps
and cricket-bats. Other boys gallop by on the
riding-master's hacks. I protest it is *Cramp,
Riding Master*, as it used to be in the reign of
George IV., and that Centaur Cramp must be
at least a hundred years old. Yonder comes
a footman with a bundle of novels from the
library. Are they as good as *our* novels ? Oh !
how delightful they were ! Shades of Valan-
cour, awful ghost of Manfroni, how I shudder
at your appearance ! Sweet image of Thaddeus
of Warsaw, how often has this almost infantile
hand tried to depict you in a Polish cap and
richly embroidered tights ! And as for Corinthian Tom in light blue pantaloons and Hes-
sians, and Jerry Hawthorn from the country,
can all the fashion, can all the splendor of

real life which these eyes have subsequently beheld, can all the wit I have heard or read in later times, compare with your fashion, with your brilliancy, with your delightful grace, and sparkling vivacious rattle?

Who knows? They *may* have kept those very books at the library still — at the well-remembered library on the Pantiles, where they sell that delightful, useful Tunbridge ware. I will go and see. I went my way to the Pantiles, the queer little old-world Pantiles, where, a hundred years since, so much good company came to take its pleasure. Is it possible that, in the past century, gentlefolks of the first rank (as I read lately in a lecture on George II. in the *Cornhill Magazine*) assembled here and entertained each other with gaming, dancing, fiddling, and tea? There are fiddlers, harpers, and trumpeters performing at this moment in a weak little old balcony, but where is the fine company? Where are the earls, duchesses, bishops, and magnificent embroidered game-sters? A half dozen of children and their nurses are listening to the musicians; an old lady or two in a poke-bonnet passes, and for the rest, I see but an uninteresting population of native tradesmen. As for the library, its window is full of pictures of burly theologians,

and their works, sermons, apologues, and so
forth.   Can I go in and ask the young ladies at
the counters for " Manfroni, or the One-Handed
Monk," and " Life in London, or the Adventures
of Corinthian Tom, Jeremiah Hawthorn, Esq.,
and their friend Bob Logic ? " — absurd.   I
turn away abashed from the casement — from
the Pantiles — no longer Pantiles, but Parade.
I stroll over the Common and survey the beautiful purple hills around, twinkling with a thousand bright villas, which have sprung up over
this charming ground since first I saw it.   What
an admirable scene of peace and plenty !   What
a delicious air breathes over the heath, blows
the cloud shadows across it, and murmurs
through the full-clad trees !   Can the world
show a land fairer, richer, more cheerful ?   I
see a portion of it when I look up from the
window at which I write.   But fair scene, green
woods, bright terraces gleaming in sunshine,
and purple clouds swollen with summer rain —
nay, the very pages over which my head bends
— disappear from before my eyes.   They are
looking backwards, back into forty years off,
into a dark room, into a little house hard by on
the Common here, in the Bartlemy-tide holidays.   The parents have gone to town for two
days : the house is all his own, his own and a

grim old maid-servant's, and a little boy is
seated at night in the lonely drawing-room,
poring over "Manfroni, or the One-Handed
Monk," so frightened that he scarcely dares to
turn round.

DE JUVENTUTE.

OUR last paper of this veracious and roundabout series related to a period which can only
be historical to a great number of readers of
this Magazine. Four I saw at the station to-
day with orange-covered books in their hands,
who can but have known George IV. by books,
and statues, and pictures. Elderly gentlemen
were in their prime, old men in their middle
age, when he reigned over us. His image remains on coins ; on a picture or two hanging
here and there in a Club or old-fashioned dining-
room ; on horseback, as at Trafalgar Square,
for example, where I defy any monarch to look
more uncomfortable. He turns up in sundry
memoirs and histories which may have been
published in Mr. Massey's "History ;" in the
"Buckingham and Grenville Correspondence ;"
and gentlemen who have accused a certain writer of disloyalty are referred to those volumes
to see whether the picture drawn of George is

overcharged. Charon has paddled him off ; he has mingled with the crowded republic of the dead. His effigy smiles from a canvas or two. Breechless he bestrides his steed in Trafalgar Square. I believe he still wears his robes at Madame Tussaud's (Madame herself having quitted Baker Street and life, and found him she modeled t' other side the Stygian stream). On the head of a five - shilling piece we still occasionally come upon him, with St. George, the dragon-slayer, on the other side of the coin. Ah me ! did this George slay many dragons ? Was he a brave, heroic champion, and rescuer of virgins ? Well ! well ! have you and I overcome all the dragons that assail *us ?* come alive and victorious out of all the caverns which we have entered in life, and succored, at risk of life and limb, all poor distressed persons in whose naked limbs the dragon Poverty is about to fasten his fangs, whom the dragon Crime is poisoning with his horrible breath, and about to crunch up and devour ? O my royal liege ! O my gracious prince and warrior ! *You* a champion to fight that monster ? Your feeble spear ever pierce that slimy paunch or plated back ? See how the flames come gurgling out of his red-hot brazen throat ! What a roar ! Nearer and nearer he trails, with eyes flaming like the

lamps of a railroad engine. How he squeals,
rushing out through the darkness of his tunnel!
Now he is near. Now he is *here*. And now —
what ? — lance, shield, knight, feathers, horse
and all ? O horror, horror! Next day, round
the monster's cave, there lie a few bones more.
You, who wish to keep yours in your skins, be
thankful that you are not called upon to go out
and fight dragons. Be grateful that they don't
sally out and swallow you. Keep a wise distance from their caves, lest you pay too dearly
for approaching them. Remember that years
passed, and whole districts were ravaged, before the warrior came who was able to cope
with the devouring monster. When that knight
does make his appearance, with all my heart let
us go out and welcome him with our best songs,
huzzas, and laurel wreaths, and eagerly recognize his valor and victory. But he comes only
seldom. Countless knights were slain before
St. George won the battle. In the battle of life
are we all going to try for the honors of cham-
pionship? If we can do our duty, if we can
keep our place pretty honorably through the
combat, let us say *Laus Deo!* at the end of it,
as the firing ceases, and the night falls over the
field.

The old were middle-aged, the elderly were

in their prime, then, thirty years since, when
yon royal George was still fighting the dragon.
As for you, my pretty lass, with your saucy hat
and golden tresses tumbled in your net, and
you, my spruce young gentleman in your mandarin's cap (the young folks at the country-
place where I am staying are so attired), your
parents were unknown to each other, and wore
short frocks and short jackets, at the date of
this five-shilling piece. Only to-day I met a
dog-cart crammed with children — children
with moustaches and mandarin caps — children
with saucy hats and hair-nets — children in
short frocks and knickerbockers (surely the
prettiest boy's dress that has appeared these
hundred years) — children from twenty years
of age to six ; and father, with mother by his
side, driving in front — and on father's countenance I saw that very laugh which I remember
perfectly in the time when this crown-piece
was coined — in *his* time, in King George's time,
when we were school-boys seated on the same
form. The smile was just as broad, as bright,
as jolly, as I remember it in the past — unfor-
gotten, though not seen or thought of, for how
many decades of years, and quite and instantly
familiar, though so long out of sight.

Any contemporary of that coin who takes it up

and reads the inscription round the laureled head, "Georgius IV. Britanniarum Rex. Fid. Def. 1823," if he will but look steadily enough at the round, and utter the proper incantation, I dare say may conjure back his life there. Look well, my elderly friend, and tell me what you see ? First, I see a Sultan, with hair, beautiful hair, and a crown of laurels round his head, and his name is Georgius Rex. Fid. Def., and so on. Now the Sultan has disappeared ; and what is it that I see ? A boy, — a boy in a jacket. He is at a desk ; he has great books before him, Latin and Greek books and dictionaries. Yes, but behind the great books, which he pretends to read, is a little one, with pictures, which he is really reading. It is — yes, I can read now — it is the "Heart of Mid Lothian," by the author of "Waverley" — or, no, it is "Life in London, or the Adventures of Corinthian Tom, Jeremiah Hawthorn, and their friend Bob Logic," by Pierce Egan ; and it has pictures — oh ! such funny pictures ! As he reads, there comes behind the boy, a man, a dervish, in a black gown, like a woman, and a black square cap, and he has a book in each hand, and he seizes the boy who is reading the picture-book, and lays his head upon one of his books, and smacks it with the other. The boy makes faces, and so that picture disappears.

Now the boy has grown bigger. *He* has got on a black gown and cap, something like the dervish. He is at a table, with ever so many bottles on it, and fruit, and tobacco ; and other young dervishes come in. They seem as if they were singing. To them enters an old moollah, he takes down their names, and orders them all to go to bed. What is this ? a carriage, with four beautiful horses all galloping — a man in red is blowing a trumpet. Many young men are on the carriage — one of them is driving the horses. Surely they won't drive into that ? — ah ! they have all disappeared. And now I see one of the young men alone. He is walking in a street — a dark street — presently a light comes to a window. There is the shadow of a lady who passes. He stands there till the light goes out. Now he is in a room scribbling on a piece of paper, and kissing a miniature every now and then. There seem to be lines each pretty much of a length. I can read *heart*, *smart*, *dart* ; *Mary*, *fairy* ; *Cupid*, *stupid* ; *true*, *you* ; and never mind what more. Bah ! it is bosh. Now see, he has got a gown on again, and a wig of white hair on his head, and he is sitting with other dervishes in a great room full of them, and on a throne in the middle is an old Sultan in scarlet, sitting before a desk, and he wears a wig too — and the young man gets up and speaks to him. And now what is here ? He is in a room with ever so many children, and the miniature hanging up. Can it be a likeness of that woman who is sitting before that copper urn with a silver vase in her hand, from which she is pouring hot liquor into cups ? Was *she* ever a fairy ? She is as fat as a hippopotamus now. He is sitting on a divan by the fire. He has a paper on his knees. Read the name. It is the *Superfine Review*. It inclines to think that Mr. Dickens is not a true gentleman, that Mr. Thackeray is not a true gentleman, and that when the one is pert and the other arch, we, the gentlemen of the *Superfine Review*, think, and think rightly, that we have some cause to be indignant. The great cause why modern humor and modern sentimentalism repels us, is that they are unwarrantably familiar. Now, Mr. Sterne, the *Superfine Reviewer* thinks, " was a true sentimentalist, because he was *above all things* a true gentleman." The flattering inference is obvious ; let us be thankful for an elegant moralist watching over us, and learn, if not too old, to imitate his high-bred politeness and catch his

unobtrusive grace. If we are unwarrantably
familiar, we know who is not. If we repel by
pertness, we know who never does. If our language offends, we know who is always modest.
O pity! The vision has disappeared off the
silver, the images of youth and the past are
vanishing away! We who have lived before
railways were made belong to another world.
In how many hours could the Prince of Wales
drive from Brighton to London, with a light
carriage built expressly, and relays of horses
longing to gallop the next stage? Do you
remember Sir Somebody, the coachman of the
Age, who took our half-crown so affably? It
was only yesterday; but what a gulf between
now and then! *Then* was the old world. Stage-
coaches, more or less swift, riding-horses, pack-
horses, highwaymen, knights in armor, Norman
invaders, Roman legions, Druids, Ancient
Britons painted blue, and so forth — all these
belong to the old period. I will concede a halt
in the midst of it, and allow that gunpowder
and printing tended to modernize the world.
But your railroad starts the new era, and we of
a certain age belong to the new time and the
old one. We are of the time of chivalry as
well as the Black Prince or Sir Walter Manny.
We are of the age of steam. We have stepped

out of the old world on to "Brunel's" vast
deck, and across the waters *ingens patet tellus.*
Towards what new continent are we wending ?
to what new laws, new manners, new politics,
vast new expanses of liberties unknown as yet,
or only surmised ?   I used to know a man who
had invented a flying-machine. "Sir," he would
say, "give me but five hundred pounds, and I
will make it.   It is so simple of construction
that I tremble daily lest some other person
should light upon and patent my discovery."
Perhaps faith was wanting ; perhaps the five
hundred pounds.   He is dead, and somebody
else must make the flying-machine.   But that
will only be a step forward on the journey
already begun since we quitted the old world.
There it lies on the other side of yonder embankments.   You young folks have never seen
it ; and Waterloo is to you no more than Agin-
court, and George IV. than Sardanapalus.   We
elderly people have lived in that pre-railroad
world, which has passed into limbo and van-
ished from under us.   I tell you it was firm under our feet once, and not long ago.   They have
raised those railroad embankments up, and shut
off the old world that was behind them.   Climb
up that bank on which the irons are laid, and
look to the other side — it is gone.   There *is*

no other side. Try and catch yesterday. Where is it ? Here is a *Times* newspaper, dated Monday 26th, and this is Tuesday 27th. Suppose you deny there was such a day as yesterday.

We who lived before railways, and survive out of the ancient world, are like Father Noah and his family out of the Ark. The children will gather round and say to us patriarchs, "'Tell us, grandpapa, about the old world." And we shall mumble our old stories ; and we shall drop off one by one ; and there will be fewer and fewer of us, and these very old and feeble. There will be but ten pre-railroadites left ; then three — then two — then one — then 0 ! If the hippopotamus had the least sensibility (of which I cannot trace any signs either in his hide or his face), I think he would go down to the bottom of his tank, and never come up again. Does he not see that he belongs to bygone ages, and that his great hulking barrel of a body is out of place in these times ? What has he in common with the brisk young life surrounding him ? In the watches of the night, when the keepers are asleep, when the birds are on one leg, when even the little armadillo is quiet, and the monkeys have ceased their chatter, — he, I mean the hippopotamus, and the elephant, and the long-necked giraffe, perhaps may lay their heads together and have a colloquy about the great silent antediluvian world which they remember, where mighty monsters floundered through the ooze, crocodiles basked on the banks, and dragons darted out of the caves and waters before men were made to slay them. We who lived before railways are antediluvians — we must pass away. We are growing scarcer every day ; and old — old — very old relicts of the times when George was still fighting the Dragon.

Not long since, a company of horse-riders paid a visit to our watering-place. We went to see them, and I bethought me that young Walter Juvenis, who was in the place, might like also to witness the performance. A pantomime is not always amusing to persons who have attained a certain age ; but a boy at a pantomime is always amused and amusing, and to see his pleasure is good for most hypochondriacs.

We sent to Walter's mother, requesting that he might join us, and the kind lady replied that the boy had already been at the morning performance of the equestrians, but was most eager to go in the evening likewise. And go he did ; and laughed at all Mr. Merryman's remarks, though he remembered them with remarkable

accuracy, and insisted upon waiting to the very
end of the fun, and was only induced to retire
just before its conclusion by representations
that the ladies of the party would be incom-
moded if they were to wait and undergo the
rush and trample of the crowd round about.
When this fact was pointed out to him, he
yielded at once, though with a heavy heart, his
eyes looking longingly towards the ring as we
retreated out of the booth. We were scarcely
clear of the place, when we heard "God save
the queen," played by the equestrian band, the
signal that all was over. Our companion entertained us with scraps of the dialogue on our
way home — precious crumbs of wit which he
had brought away from that feast. He laughed
over them again as we walked under the stars.
He has them now, and takes them out of the
pocket of his memory, and crunches a bit, and
relishes it with sentimental tenderness, too, for
he is, no doubt, back at school by this time ; the
holidays are over ; and Doctor Birch's young
friends have reassembled.

Queer jokes, which caused a thousand simple
mouths to grin ! As the jaded Merryman uttered them to the old gentleman with the whip,
some of the old folks in the audience, I dare
say, indulged in reflections of their own. There

was one joke — I utterly forget it — but it
began with Merryman saying what he had for
dinner. He had mutton for dinner, at one
o'clock, after which " he had to *come to business*."
And then came the point. Walter Juvenis,
Esq., Rev. Doctor Birch's, Market Rodborough,
if you read this will you please send me a line,
and let me know what was the joke Mr. Merryman told about having his dinner? *You* remember well enough. But do I want to know?
Suppose a boy takes a favorite long cherished
lump of cake out of his pocket, and offers you
a bite? *Merci!* The fact is, I don't care
much about knowing that joke of Mr. Merryman's.

But whilst he was talking about his dinner,
and his mutton, and his landlord, and his business, I felt a great interest about Mr. M. in
private life — about his wife, lodgings, earn-
ings, and general history, and I dare say was
forming a picture of those in my mind : — wife
cooking the mutton : children waiting for it !
Merryman in his plain clothes, and so forth ;
during which contemplation the joke was uttered and laughed at, and Mr. M., resuming his
professional duties, was tumbling over head
and heels. Do not suppose I am going, *sicut
est mos*, to indulge in moralities about buffoons,

paint, motley, and mountebanking. Nay, Prime
Ministers rehearse their jokes; Opposition
leaders prepare and polish them; Tabernacle
preachers must arrange them in their minds
before they utter them. All I mean is, that I
would like to know any one of these perform-
ers thoroughly, and out of his uniform: that
preacher, and why in his travels this and that
point struck him; wherein lies his power of
pathos, humor, eloquence; — that Minister of
State, and what moves him, and how his private
heart is working; — I would only say that at a
certain time of life certain things cease to interest; but about *some* things when we cease
to care, what will be the use of life, sight, hearing? Poems are written, and we cease to admire. Lady Jones invites us, and we yawn; she
ceases to invite us, and we are resigned. The
last time I saw a ballet at the opera — oh! it
is many years ago — I fell asleep in the stalls
wagging my head in insane dreams, and I hope
affording amusement to the company, while the
feet of five hundred nymphs were cutting flic-
flacs on the stage at a few paces' distance. Ah!
I remember a different state of things! *Credite
posteri.* To see those nymphs — gracious powers,
how beautiful they were! That leering, painted,
shriveled, thin-armed, thick-ankled old thing,

cutting dreary capers, coming thumping down
on her board out of time — *that* an opera-dan-
cer? Pooh! My dear Walter, the great difference between *my* time and yours, who will
enter life some two or three years hence, is
that, now, the dancing women and singing
women are ludicrously old, out of time, and out
of tune ; the paint is so visible, and the dinge
and wrinkles of their wretched old cotton
stockings, that I am surprised how anybody
can like to look at them. And as for laughing
at *me* for falling asleep, I can't understand a
man of sense doing otherwise. In *my* time, *à
la bonne heure.* In the reign of George IV., I
give you my honor, all the dancers at the opera
were as beautiful as houries. Even in William
IV.'s time, when I think of Duvernay prancing
in as the Bayadère, — I say it was a vision of
loveliness such as mortal eyes can't see nowadays. How well I remember the tune to which
she used to appear ! Kaled used to say to the
Sultan, " My lord, a troop of those dancing and
singing gurls called Bayadères approaches,"
and, to the clash of cymbals, and the thumping
of my heart, in she used to dance ! There has
never been anything like it — never. There
never will be — I laugh to scorn old people
who tell me about your Noblet, your Montessu,

your Vestris, your Parisot — pshaw, the senile twaddlers! And the impudence of the young men with their music and their dances of to-day! I tell you the women are dreary old creatures. I tell you one air in an opera is just like another, and they send all rational creatures to sleep. Ah, Ronzi de Begnis, thou lovely one! Ah, Caradori, thou smiling angel! Ah, Malibran! Nay, I will come to modern times, and acknowledge that Lablache was a very good singer thirty years ago (though Porto was the boy for me) : and then we had Ambrogetti, and Curioni, and Donzelli, a rising young singer.

But what is most certain and lamentable is the decay of stage beauty since the days of George IV. Think of Sontag! I remember her in *Otello* and the *Donna del Lago* in '28. I remember being behind the scenes at the opera (where numbers of us young fellows of fashion used to go), and seeing Sontag let her hair fall down over her shoulders previous to her murder by Donzelli. Young fellows have never seen beauty like *that*, heard such a voice, seen such hair, such eyes. Don't tell *me!* A man who has been about town since the reign of George IV., ought he not to know better than you young lads who have seen nothing?

The deterioration of women is lamentable ; and the conceit of the young fellows more lamentable still, that they won't see this fact, but persist in thinking their time as good as ours.

Bless me ! when I was a lad, the stage was covered with angels, who sang, acted, and danced. When I remember the Adelphi, and the actresses there ; when I think of Miss Chester, and Miss Love, and Mrs. Serle at Sadler's Wells, and her forty glorious pupils — of the Opera and Noblet, and the exquisite young Taglioni, and Pauline Leroux, and a host more ! One much-admired being of those days I confess I never cared for, and that was the chief *male* dancer — a very important personage then, with a bare neck, bare arms, a tunic, and a hat and feathers, who used to divide the applause with the ladies, and who has now sunk down a trap-door forever. And this frank admission ought to show that I am not your mere twaddling *laudator temporis acti* — your old fogy who can see no good except in his own time.

They say that claret is better nowadays, and cookery much improved since the time of *my* monarch — of George IV. *Pastry Cookery* is certainly not so good. I have often eaten half a crown's worth (including, I trust, gingerbeer) at our school pastry-cook's, and that is a proof that the pastry must have been very good, for could I do as much now? I passed by the pastry-cook's shop lately, having occasion to visit my old school. It looked a very dingy old baker's; misfortunes may have come over him — those penny tarts certainly did *not* look so nice as I remember them: but he may have grown careless as he has grown old (I should judge him to be now about ninety-six years of age), and his hand may have lost its cunning.

Not that we were not great epicures. I remember how we constantly grumbled at the quantity of the food in our master's house — which on my conscience I believe was excellent and plentiful — and how we tried once or twice to eat him out of house and home. At the pastry-cook's we may have over-eaten ourselves (I have admitted half a crown's worth for my own part, but I don't like to mention the *real* figure for fear of perverting the present generation of boys by my monstrous confession) — we may have eaten too much, I say. We did; but what then? The school apothecary was sent for: a couple of small globules at night, a trifling preparation of senna in the morning, and we had not to go to school, so that the draught was an actual pleasure.

For our amusements, besides the games in

vogue, which were pretty much in old times as
they are now (except cricket, *par exemple* —
and I wish the present youth joy of their
bowling, and suppose Armstrong and Whitworth
will bowl at them with light field-pieces next),
there were novels — ah! I trouble you to find
such novels in the present day! O Scottish
Chiefs, did n't we weep over you! O Mysteries
of Udolpho, did n't I and Briggs Minor draw
pictures out of you, as I have said? Efforts,
feeble indeed, but still giving pleasure to us
and our friends. "I say, old boy, draw us
Vivaldi tortured in the Inquisition," or "Draw
us Don Quixote and the windmills, you know,"
amateurs would say, to boys who had a love of
drawing. "Peregrine Pickle" we liked, our
fathers admiring it, and telling us (the sly old
boys) it was capital fun; but I think I was
rather bewildered by it, though "Roderick
Random" was and remains delightful. I don't
remember having Sterne in the school library,
no doubt because the works of that divine were
not considered decent for young people. Ah!
not against thy genius, O father of Uncle Toby
and Trim, would I say a word in disrespect.
But I am thankful to live in times when men
no longer have the temptation to write so as
to call blushes on women's cheeks, and would

shame to whisper wicked allusions to honest
boys. Then, above all, we had WALTER SCOTT,
the kindly, the generous, the pure — the companion of what countless delightful hours; the
purveyor of how much happiness; the friend
whom we recall as the constant benefactor of
our youth! How well I remember the type
and the brownish paper of the old duodecimo
"Tales of my Landlord"! I have never dared
to read the "Pirate," and the "Bride of Lam-
mermoor," or "Kenilworth," from that day to
this because the finale is unhappy, and people
die, and are murdered at the end. But "Ivanhoe," and "Quentin Durward"! Oh! for a
half-holiday, and a quiet corner, and one of
those books again! Those books, and perhaps
those eyes with which we read them; and it
may be, the brains behind the eyes! It may
be the tart was good; but how fresh the appetite was! If the gods would give me the
desire of my heart, I should be able to write a
story which boys would relish for the next few
dozen of centuries. The boy-critic loves the
story: grown up, he loves the author who wrote
the story. Hence the kindly tie is established
between writer and reader, and lasts pretty
nearly for life. I meet people now who don't
care for Walter Scott, or the "Arabian Nights;"

I am sorry for them, unless they in their time have found *their* romancer — their charming Scheherazade. By the way, Walter, when you are writing, tell me who is the favorite novelist in the fourth form now? Have you got anything so good and kindly as dear Miss Edgeworth's *Frank?* It used to belong to a fellow's sisters generally ; but though he pretended to despise it, and said " Oh, stuff for girls ! " he read it ; and I think there were one or two passages which would try my eyes now, were I to meet with the little book.

As for Thomas and Jeremiah (it is only my witty way of calling Tom and Jerry), I went to the British Museum the other day on purpose to get it ; but somehow, if you will press the question so closely, on reperusal, Tom and Jerry is not so brilliant as I had supposed it to be. The pictures are just as fine as ever ; and I shook hands with broad-backed Jerry Hawthorn and Corinthian Tom with delight, after many years' absence. But the style of the writing, I own, was not pleasing to me ; I even thought it a little vulgar — well ! well ! other writers have been considered vulgar — and as a description of the sports and amusements of London in the ancient times, more curious than amusing.

But the pictures!—oh! the pictures are noble still! First, there is Jerry arriving from the country, in a green coat and leather gaiters, and being measured for a fashionable suit at Corinthian House, by Corinthian Tom's tailor. Then away for the career of pleasure and fashion. The park! delicious excitement! The theatre! the saloon!! the green room!!! Rapturous bliss—the opera itself! and then perhaps to Temple Bar, to *knock down a Charley* there! There are Jerry and Tom, with their tights and little cocked hats, coming from the opera—very much as gentlemen in waiting on royalty are habited now. There they are at Almack's itself, amidst a crowd of high-bred personages, with the Duke of Clarence himself looking at them dancing. Now, strange change, they are in Tom Cribb's parlor, where they don't seem to be a whit less at home than in fashion's gilded halls: and now they are at Newgate, seeing the irons knocked off the malefactor's legs previous to execution. What hardened ferocity in the countenance of the desperado in yellow breeches! What compunction in the face of the gentleman in black (who, I suppose, had been forging), and who clasps his hands, and listens to the chaplain! Now we haste away to merrier scenes: to

Tattersall's (ah gracious powers ! what a funny
fellow that actor was who performed Dicky
Green in that scene at the play !) ; and now we
are at a private party, at which Corinthian Tom
is waltzing (and very gracefully, too, as you
must confess) with Corinthian Kate, whilst Bob
Logic, the Oxonian, is playing on the piano !

"After," the text says, "*the Oxonian* had
played several pieces of lively music, he re-
quested as a favor that Kate and his friend
Tom would perform a waltz.   Kate without
any hesitation immediately stood up.   Tom
offered his hand to his fascinating partner, and
the dance took place.   The plate conveys a
correct representation of the 'gay scene' at
that precise moment.   The anxiety of *the Oxonian* to witness the attitudes of the elegant
pair had nearly put a stop to their movements.
On turning round from the pianoforte and pre-
senting his comical *mug*, Kate could scarcely
suppress a laugh."

And no wonder ; just look at it now (as I
have copied it to the best of my humble ability),
and compare Master Logic's countenance and
attitude with the splendid elegance of Tom !
Now every London man is weary and *blasé*.
There is an enjoyment of life in these young
bucks of 1823 which contrasts strangely with

our feelings of 1860. Here, for instance, is a specimen of their talk and walk. "'If,' says LOGIC — 'if *enjoyment* is your *motto*, you may make the most of an evening at Vauxhall, more than at any other place in the metropolis. It is all free and easy. Stay as long as you like, and depart when you think proper.' — 'Your description is so flattering,' replied JERRY, 'that I do not care how soon the time arrives for us to start.' LOGIC proposed a '*bit of a stroll*' in order to get rid of an hour or two, which was immediately accepted by Tom and Jerry. A *turn* or two in Bond Street, a *stroll* through Piccadilly, a *look in* at TATTERSALL'S, a *ramble* through Pall Mall, and a *strut* on the Corinthian path, fully occupied the time of our heroes until the hour for dinner arrived, when a few glasses of TOM'S rich wines soon put them on the *qui vive*. VAUXHALL was then the object in view, and the TRIO started, bent upon enjoying the pleasures which this place so amply affords."

How nobly those inverted commas, those italics, those capitals, bring out the writer's wit and relieve the eye! They are as good as jokes, though you mayn't quite perceive the point. Mark the varieties of lounge in which the young men indulge — now *a stroll*, then *a*

look in, then *a ramble,* and presently *a strut.*
When George, Prince of Wales, was twenty, I
have read in an old Magazine, "the Prince's
lounge" was a peculiar manner of walking
which the young bucks imitated.   At Windsor
George III. had *a cat's path* — a sly early walk
which the good old king took in the gray morning before his household was astir.   What was
the Corinthian path here recorded ?   Does any
antiquary know ?   And what were the rich
wines which our friends took, and which enabled them to enjoy Vauxhall ?   Vauxhall is
gone, but the wines which could occasion such
a delightful perversion of the intellect as to
enable it to enjoy ample pleasures there, what
were they ?

So the game of life proceeds, until Jerry
Hawthorn, the rustic, is fairly knocked up by
all this excitement and is forced to go home,
and the last picture represents him getting into
the coach at the "White Horse Cellar," he
being one of six inside, whilst his friends shake
him by the hand ; whilst the sailor mounts on
the roof ; whilst the Jews hang round with
oranges, knives, and sealing-wax : whilst the
guard is closing the door.   Where are they
now, those sealing-wax venders ?   where are
the guards ?   where are the jolly teams ?   where

are the coaches? and where the youth that
climbed inside and out of them; that heard the
merry horn which sounds no more; that saw
the sun rise over Stonehenge; that rubbed
away the bitter tears at night after parting as
the coach sped on the journey to school and
London; that looked out with beating heart as
the milestones flew by, for the welcome corner
where began home and holidays?

It is night now: and here is home. Gathered
under the quiet roof elders and children lie
alike at rest. In the midst of a great peace
and calm, the stars look out from the heavens.
The silence is peopled with the past; sorrowful
remorses for sins and shortcomings — memories
of passionate joys and griefs rise out of their
graves, both now alike calm and sad. Eyes, as
I shut mine, look at me, that have long ceased
to shine. The town and the fair landscapes
sleep under the starlight, wreathed in the
autumn mists. Twinkling among the houses a
light keeps watch here and there, in what may
be a sick-chamber or two. The clock tolls
sweetly in the silent air. Here is night and
rest. An awful sense of thanks makes the
heart swell, and the head bow, as I pass to my
room through the sleeping house, and feel as
though a hushed blessing were upon it.

ROUND ABOUT THE CHRISTMAS-TREE.

THE kindly Christmas-tree, from which I trust every gentle reader has pulled a bonbon or two, is yet all aflame whilst I am writing, and sparkles with the sweet fruits of its season. You young ladies, may you have plucked pretty giftlings from it; and out of the cracker sugar-plum which you have split with the captain or the sweet young curate may you have read one of those delicious conundrums which the confectioners introduce into the sweetmeats, and which apply to the cunning passion of love. Those riddles are to be read at *your* age, when I dare say they are amusing. As for Dolly, Merry, and Bell, who are standing at the tree, they don't care about the love-riddle part, but understand the sweet-almond portion very well. They are four, five, six years old. Patience, little people! A dozen merry Christmases more, and you will be reading those wonderful love-conundrums, too. As for us elderly folks, we watch the babies at their sport, and the young people pulling at the branches : and instead of finding bonbons or sweeties in the packets which *we* pluck off the boughs, we find enclosed Mr. Carnifex's review of the quarter's meat ; Mr. Sartor's compliments, and little statement for self and the young gentlemen ; and Madame de Sainte-Crinoline's respects to the young ladies, who encloses her account, and will send on Saturday, please ; or we stretch our hand out to the educational branch of the Christmas - tree,* and there find a lively and amusing article from the Rev. Henry Holyshade, containing our dear Tommy's exceedingly moderate account for the last term's school expenses.

The tree yet sparkles, I say. I am writing on the day before Twelfth Day, if you must know ; but already ever so many of the fruits have been pulled, and the Christmas lights have gone out. Bobby Miseltow, who has been staying with us for a week (and who has been sleeping mysteriously in the bathroom), comes to say he is going away to spend the rest of the holidays with his grandmother — and I brush away the manly tears of regret as I part with the dear child. "Well, Bob, good-by, since you *will* go. Compliments to grandmamma. Thank her for the turkey. Here's " — (*A slight pecuniary transaction takes place at this juncture, and Bob nods and winks, and puts his hand in his waistcoat pocket.*) "You have had a pleasant week ? "

BOB. — " Have n't I ! " (*And exit, anxious to know the amount of coin which has just changed hands.*)

He is gone, and as the dear boy vanishes through the door (behind which I see him perfectly), I too cast up a little account of our past Christmas week. When Bob's holidays are over, and the printer has sent me back this manuscript, I know Christmas will be an old story. All the fruit will be off the Christmas-tree then ; the crackers will have cracked off ; the almonds will have been crunched ; and the sweet-bitter riddles will have been read ; the lights will have perished off the dark green boughs ; the toys growing on them will have been distributed, fought for, cherished, neglected, broken. Ferdinand and Fidelia will each keep out of it (be still, my gushing heart!) the remembrance of a riddle read together, of a double-almond munched together, and the moiety of an exploded cracker. . . . The maids, I say, will have taken down all that holly stuff and nonsense about the clocks, lamps, and looking-glasses, the dear boys will be back at school, fondly thinking of the pantomime-fairies whom they have seen ; whose gaudy gossamer wings are battered by this time ; and whose pink cotton (or silk is it ?)

lower extremities are all dingy and dusty. Yet
but a few days, Bob, and flakes of paint will
have cracked off the fairy flower-bowers, and
the revolving temples of adamantine lustre will
be as shabby as the city of Pekin. When you
read this, will Clown still be going on lolling
his tongue out of his mouth, and saying, "How
are you to-morrow?" To-morrow, indeed!
He must be almost ashamed of himself (if that
cheek is still capable of the blush of shame) for
asking the absurd question. To-morrow, indeed! To-morrow the diffugient snows will
give place to Spring; the snowdrops will lift
their heads; Ladyday may be expected, and
the pecuniary duties peculiar to that feast; in
place of bonbons, trees will have an eruption of
light green knobs; the white bait season will
bloom . . . as if one need go on describing
these vernal phenomena, when Christmas is still
here, though ending, and the subject of my dis-
course!

We have all admired the illustrated papers,
and noted how boisterously jolly they become
at Christmas time. What wassail-bowls, robin-
redbreasts, waits, snow landscapes, bursts of
Christmas song! And then to think that these
festivities are prepared months before — that
these Christmas pieces are prophetic! How

kind of artists and poets to devise the festivities beforehand, and serve them pat at the proper time! We ought to be grateful to them, as to the cook who gets up at midnight and sets the pudding a-boiling, which is to feast us at six o'clock. I often think with gratitude of the famous Mr. Nelson Lee — the author of I don't know how many hundred glorious pantomimes — walking by the summer wave at Margate, or Brighton perhaps, revolving in his mind the idea of some new gorgeous spectacle of faëry, which the winter shall see complete. He is like the cook at midnight (*si parva licet*). He watches and thinks. He pounds the sparkling sugar of benevolence, the plums of fancy, the sweetmeats of fun, the figs of — well, the figs of fairy fiction, let us say, and pops the whole in the seething caldron of imagination, and at due season serves up THE PANTOMIME.

Very few men in the course of nature can expect to see *all* the pantomimes in one season, but I hope to the end of my life I shall never forego reading about them in that delicious sheet of *The Times* which appears on the morning after Boxing-day. Perhaps reading is even better than seeing. The best way, I think, is to say you are ill, lie in bed, and have the paper for two hours, reading all the way down from Drury Lane to the Britannia at Hoxton. Bob and I went to two pantomimes. One was at the Theatre of Fancy, and the other at the Fairy Opera, and I don't know which we liked the best.

At the Fancy, we saw " Harlequin Hamlet, or Daddy's Ghost and Nunky's Pison," which is all very well — but, gentlemen, if you don't respect Shakespeare, to whom will you be civil ? The palace and ramparts of Elsinore by moon and snowlight is one of Loutherbourg's finest efforts. The banqueting hall of the palace is illuminated : the peaks and gables glitter with the snow : the sentinels march blowing their fingers with the cold — the freezing of the nose of one of them is very neatly and dexterously arranged : the snow storm rises : the winds howl awfully along the battlements : the waves come curling, leaping, foaming to shore. Hamlet's umbrella is whirled away in the storm. He and his two friends stamp on each other's toes to keep them warm. The storm-spirits rise in the air, and are whirled howling round the palace and the rocks. My eyes! what tiles and chimney-pots fly hurtling through the air ! As the storm reaches its height (here the wind instruments come in with prodigious effect, and I compliment Mr. Brumby and the violoncellos)

— as the snow-storm rises (queek, queek, queek, go the fiddles, and then thrumpty thrump comes a pizzicato movement in Bob Major, which sends a shiver into your very boot soles) the thunder-clouds deepen (bong, bong, bong, from the violoncellos). The forked lightning quivers through the clouds in a zigzag scream of violins — and look, look, look! as the frothing, roaring waves come rushing up the battlements, and over the reeling parapet, each hissing wave becomes a ghost, sends the gun-carriages rolling over the platform, and plunges howling into the water again.

Hamlet's mother comes on to the battlements to look for her son. The storm whips her umbrella out of her hands, and she retires screaming in pattens.

The cabs on the stand in the great market-place at Elsinore are seen to drive off, and several people are drowned. The gas-lamps along the street are wrenched from their foundations, and shoot through the troubled air. Whist, rush, hish! how the rain roars and pours! The darkness becomes awful, always deepened by the power of the music — and see — in the midst of a rush, and whirl, and scream of spirits of air and wave — what is that ghastly figure moving hither? It becomes bigger, big-

ger, as it advances down the platform — more
ghastly, more horrible, enormous! It is as tall
as the whole stage. It seems to be advancing
on the stalls and pit, and the whole house
screams with terror, as the GHOST OF THE LATE
HAMLET comes in, and begins to speak. Several
people faint, and the light-fingered gentry pick
pockets furiously in the darkness.

In the pitchy darkness, this awful figure
throwing his eyes about, the gas in the boxes
shuddering out of sight, and the wind-instru-
ments bugling the most horrible wails, the bold-
est spectator must have felt frightened. But
hark! what is that silver shimmer of the
fiddles! Is it — can it be — the gray dawn
peeping in the stormy east? The ghost's eyes
look blankly towards it, and roll a ghastly
agony. Quicker, quicker ply the violins of
Phœbus Apollo. Redder, redder grow the
orient clouds. Cockadoodledoo! crows that
great cock which has just come out on the roof
of the palace. And now the round sun himself
pops up from behind the waves of night.
Where is the ghost? He is gone! Purple
shadows of morn "slant o'er the snowy sward,"
the city wakes up in life and sunshine, and we
confess we are very much relieved at the dis-
appearance of the ghost. We don't like those
dark scenes in pantomimes.

After the usual business, that Ophelia should be turned into Columbine was to be expected ; but I confess I was a little shocked when Hamlet's mother became Pantaloon, and was instantly knocked down by Clown Claudius. Grimaldi is getting a little old now, but for real humor there are few clowns like him. Mr. Shuter, as the grave-digger, was chaste and comic, as he always is, and the scene-painters surpassed themselves.

"Harlequin Conqueror and the field of Hastings," at the other house, is very pleasant too. The irascible William is acted with great vigor by Snoxall, and the battle of Hastings is a good piece of burlesque. Some trifling liberties are taken with history, but what liberties will not the merry genius of pantomime permit himself ? At the battle of Hastings, William is on the point of being defeated by the Sussex volunteers, very elegantly led by the always pretty Miss Waddy (as Haco Sharpshooter), when a shot from the Normans kills Harold. The fairy Edith hereupon comes forward, and finds his body, which straightway leaps up a live harlequin, whilst the Conqueror makes an excellent clown, and the Archbishop of Bayeux a diverting pantaloon, etc., etc., etc.

Perhaps these are not the pantomimes we

really saw; but one description will do as well
as another. The plots, you see, are a little in-
tricate and difficult to understand in pantomimes; and I may have mixed up one with
another. That I was at the theatre on Boxing-
night is certain — but the pit was so full that I
could only see fairy legs glittering in the distance, as I stood at the door. And if I was
badly off, I think there was a young gentleman
behind me worse off still. I own that he has
good reason (though others have not) to speak
ill of me behind my back, and hereby beg his
pardon.

Likewise to the gentleman who picked up a
party in Piccadilly, who had slipped and fallen
in the snow, and was there on his back, uttering
energetic expressions; that party begs to offer
thanks, and compliments of the season.

Bob's behavior on New Year's day, I can
assure Dr. Holyshade, was highly creditable to
the boy. He had expressed a determination to
partake of every dish which was put on the
table; but after soup, fish, roast-beef, and roast-
goose, he retired from active business until the
pudding and mince-pies made their appearance,
of which he partook liberally, but not too freely.
And he greatly advanced in my good opinion
by praising the punch, which was of my own

manufacture, and which some gentlemen present (Mr. O'M—g—n, amongst others) pronounced to be too weak. Too weak! A bottle of rum, a bottle of Madeira, half a bottle of brandy, and two bottles and a half of water — *can* this mixture be said to be too weak for any mortal? Our young friend amused the company during the evening by exhibiting a two-shilling magic-lantern, which he had purchased, and likewise by singing "Sally, come up!" a quaint, but rather monotonous melody, which I am told is sung by the poor negro on the banks of the broad Mississippi.

What other enjoyments did we proffer for the child's amusement during the Christmas week? A great philosopher was giving a lecture to young folks at the British Institution. But when this diversion was proposed to our young friend Bob, he said, " Lecture? no, thank you. Not as I knows on," and made sarcastic signals on his nose. Perhaps he is of Dr. Johnson's opinion about lectures : " Lectures, sir ! what man would go to hear that imperfectly at a lecture, which he can read at leisure in a book ? " *I* never went, of my own choice, to a lecture ; that I can vow. As for sermons, they are different ; I delight in them, and they cannot, of course, be too long.

Well, we partook of yet other Christmas
delights besides pantomime, pudding, and pie.
One glorious, one delightful, one most unlucky
and pleasant day, we drove in a brougham, with
a famous horse, which carried us more quickly
and briskly than any of your vulgar railways,
over Battersea Bridge, on which the horse's
hoofs rung as if it had been iron ; through sub-
urban villages, plum-caked with snow ; under
a leaden sky, in which the sun hung like a red-
hot warming-pan ; by pond after pond, where
not only men and boys, but scores after scores
of women and girls, were sliding, and roaring,
and clapping their lean old sides with laughter,
as they tumbled down, and their hobnailed
shoes flew up in the air ; the air frosty with a
lilac haze, through which villas, and commons,
and churches, and plantations glimmered. We
drive up the hill, Bob and I ; we make the last
two miles in eleven minutes ; we pass that poor,
armless man who sits there in the cold, following you with his eyes. I don't give anything,
and Bob looks disappointed. We are set down
neatly at the gate, and a horse-holder opens the
brougham door. I don't give anything ; again
disappointment on Bob's part. I pay a shilling apiece, and we enter into the glorious
building, which is decorated for Christmas, and

straightway forgetfulness on Bob's part of
everything but that magnificent scene. The
enormous edifice is all decorated for Bob and
Christmas. The stalls, the columns, the fountains, courts, statues, splendors, are all crowned
for Christmas. The delicious negro is singing
his Alabama choruses for Christmas and Bob.
He has scarcely done, when, Tootarootatoo !
Mr. Punch is performing his surprising actions,
and hanging the beadle. The stalls are decorated. The refreshment-tables are piled with
good things ; at many fountains "MULLED
CLARET" is written up in appetizing capitals,
"Mulled Claret — oh, jolly ! How cold it is ! "
says Bob ; I pass on. "It's only three o'clock,"
says Bob. "No, only three," I say meekly.
"We dine at seven," sighs Bob, "and it 's so-o-o
coo-old." I still would take no hints. No
claret, no refreshment, no sandwiches, no sau-
sage rolls for Bob. At last I am obliged to
tell him all. Just before we left home, a little
Christmas bill popped in at the door and
emptied my purse at the threshold. I forgot
all about the transaction, and had to borrow
half a crown from John Coachman to pay for
our entrance into the palace of delight. *Now*
you see, Bob, why I could not treat you on that
second of January when we drove to the pal-

ace together; when the girls and boys were sliding on the ponds at Dulwich; when the darkling river was full of floating ice, and the sun was like a warming-pan in the leaden sky.

One more Christmas sight we had, of course; and that sight I think I like as well as Bob himself at Christmas, and at all seasons. We went to a certain garden of delight where, whatever your cares are, I think you can manage to forget some of them, and muse, and be not unhappy; to a garden beginning with a Z, which is as lively as Noah's ark; where the fox has brought his brush, and the cock has brought his comb, and the elephant has brought his trunk, and the kangaroo has brought his bag, and the condor his old white wig and black satin hood. On this day it was so cold that the white bears winked their pink eyes, as they plapped up and down by their pool, and seemed to say, "Aha, this weather reminds us of our dear home!" "Cold! bah! I have got such a warm coat," says brother Bruin, "I don't mind;" and he laughs on his pole, and clucks down a bun. The squealing hyænas gnashed their teeth and laughed at us quite refreshingly at their window; and, cold as it was, Tiger, Tiger, burning bright, glared at us red-hot

through his bars, and snorted blasts of hell.
The woolly camel leered at us quite kindly as
he paced round his rings on his silent pads.
We went to our favorite places. Our dear
wombat came up, and had himself scratched
very affably. Our fellow-creatures in the
monkey-room held out their little black hands,
and piteously asked us for Christmas alms.
Those darling alligators on their rock winked
at us in the most friendly way. The solemn
eagles sat alone, and scowled at us from their
peaks ; whilst little Tom Ratel tumbled over
head and heels for us in his usual diverting
manner. If I have cares in my mind, I come
to the Zoo, and fancy they don't pass the gate.
I recognize my friends, my enemies, in countless cages. I entertained the eagle, the vulture,
the old billy-goat, and the black-pated, crimson-
necked, blear-eyed, baggy, hook-beaked old
marabou stork yesterday at dinner ; and when
Bob's aunt came to tea in the evening, and
asked him what he had seen, he stepped up to
her gravely, and said —

" First I saw the white bear, then I saw the black,
Then I saw the camel with a hump upon his back.

Chorus of Children.

" Then I saw the camel with a HUMP upon his back !
Then I saw the gray wolf, with mutton in his maw ;

Then I saw the wombat waddle in the straw ;
Then I saw the elephant with his waving trunk,
Then I saw the monkeys — mercy, how unpleasantly they
smelt ! ''

There. No one can beat that piece of wit, can
he, Bob ? And so it is all over ; but we had
a jolly time, whilst you were with us, had n't
we ? Present my respects to the doctor ; and
I hope, my boy, we may spend another merry
Christmas next year.

ON BEING FOUND OUT.

AT the close (let us say) of Queen Anne's
reign, when I was a boy at a private and pre-
paratory school for young gentlemen, I remember the wiseacre of a master ordering us
all, one night, to march into a little garden at
the back of the house, and thence to proceed
one by one into a tool or hen house (I was
but a tender little thing just put into short
clothes, and can't exactly say whether the house
was for tools or hens), and in that house to
put our hands into a sack which stood on a
bench, a candle burning beside it. I put my
hand into the sack. My hand came out quite
black. I went and joined the other boys in

the school - room ; and all their hands were black too.

By reason of my tender age (and there are some critics who, I hope, will be satisfied by my acknowledging that I am a hundred and fifty-six next birthday) I could not understand what was the meaning of this night excursion — this candle, this tool-house, this bag of soot. I think we little boys were taken out of our sleep to be brought to the ordeal. We came, then, and showed our little hands to the master ; washed them or not — most probably, I should say, not — and so went bewildered back to bed.

Something had been stolen in the school that day ; and Mr. Wiseacre having read in a book of an ingenious method of finding out a thief by making him put his hand into a sack (which, if guilty, the rogue would shirk from doing), all we boys were subjected to the trial. Goodness knows what the lost object was, or who stole it. We all had black hands to show the master. And the thief, whoever he was, was not Found Out that time.

I wonder if the rascal is alive — an elderly scoundrel he must be by this time ; and a hoary old hypocrite, to whom an old school - fellow presents his kindest regards — parenthetically

remarking what a dreadful place that private
school was ; cold, chilblains, bad dinners, not
enough victuals, and caning awful !—Are you
alive still, I say, you nameless villain, who escaped discovery on that day of crime ? I hope
you have escaped often since, old sinner. Ah,
what a lucky thing it is, for you and me, my
man, that we are *not* found out in all our pec-
cadilloes; and that our backs can slip away
from the master and the cane !

Just consider what life would be, if every
rogue was found out, and flogged *coram populo !*
What a butchery, what an indecency, what an
endless swishing of the rod ! Don't cry out
about my misanthropy. My good friend
Mealymouth, I will trouble you to tell me, do
you go to church ? When there, do you say,
or do you not, that you are a miserable sinner,
and saying so do you believe or disbelieve it ?
If you are a M. S., don't you deserve correction, and are n't you grateful if you are to
be let off ? I say again what a blessed thing it
is that we are not all found out !

Just picture to yourself everybody who does
wrong being found out, and punished accordingly. Fancy all the boys in all the school
being whipped ; and then the assistants, and
then the head master (Dr. Badford let us call

him). Fancy the provost-marshal being tied
up, having previously superintended the correction of the whole army. After the young
gentlemen have had their turn for the faulty
exercises, fancy Dr. Lincolnsinn being taken up
for certain faults in *his* Essay and Review.
After the clergyman has cried his peccavi,
suppose we hoist up a bishop, and give him
a couple of dozen! (I see my Lord Bishop of
Double - Gloucester sitting in a very uneasy
posture on his right reverend bench.) After
we have cast off the bishop, what are we to say
to the Minister who appointed him? My Lord
Cinqwarden, it is painful to have to use personal correction to a boy of your age; but
really . . . *Siste tandem, carnifex!* The butchery is too horrible. The hand drops power-
less, appalled at the quantity of birch which
it must cut and brandish. I am glad we are
not all found out, I say again; and protest,
my dear brethren, against our having our de-
serts.

To fancy all men found out and punished is
bad enough; but imagine all the women found
out in the distinguished social circle in which
you and I have the honor to move. Is it not a
mercy that a many of these fair criminals remain unpunished and undiscovered! There is

Mrs. Longbow, who is forever practicing, and who shoots poisoned arrows, too; when you meet her you don't call her liar, and charge her with the wickedness she has done and is doing. There is Mrs. Painter, who passes for a most respectable woman, and a model in society. There is no use in saying what you really know regarding her and her goings on. There is Diana Hunter — what a little haughty prude it is ; and yet *we* know stories about her which are not altogether edifying. I say it is best for the sake of the good, that the bad should not all be found out. You don't want your children to know the history of that lady in the next box, who is so handsome, and whom they admire so. Ah me, what would life be if we were all found out and punished for all our faults ? Jack Ketch would be in permanence ; and then who would hang Jack Ketch ?

They talk of murderers being pretty certainly found out. Psha! I have heard an authority awfully competent vow and declare that scores and hundreds of murders are committed, and nobody is the wiser. That terrible man mentioned one or two ways of committing murder, which he maintained were quite common, and were scarcely ever found out. A man, for instance, comes home to his wife, and

. . . but I pause — I know that this Magazine has a very large circulation. Hundreds and hundreds of thousands — why not say a million of people at once ? — well, say a million, read it. And amongst these countless readers, I might be teaching some monster how to make away with his wife without being found out, some fiend of a woman how to destroy her dear husband. I will *not* then tell this easy and simple way of murder, as communicated to me by a most respectable party in the confidence of private intercourse. Suppose some gentle reader were to try this most simple and easy receipt — it seems to me almost infallible — and come to grief in consequence, and be found out and hanged ? Should I ever pardon myself for having been the means of doing injury to a single one of our esteemed subscribers ? The prescription whereof I speak — that is to say, whereof I *don't* speak — shall be buried in this bosom. No, I am a humane man. I am not one of your Bluebeards to go and say to my wife, " My dear ! I am going away for a few days to Brighton. Here are all the keys of the house. You may open every door and closet, except the one at the end of the oak-room opposite the fireplace, with the little bronze Shakespeare on the mantelpiece (or what not)." I

don't say this to a woman — unless, to be sure,
I want to get rid of her — because, after such a
caution, I know she 'll peep into the closet. I
say nothing about the closet at all. I keep the
key in my pocket, and a being whom I love,
but who, as I know, has many weaknesses, out
of harm's way. You toss up your head, dear
angel, drub on the ground with your lovely little feet, on the table with your sweet rosy
fingers, and cry, "Oh, sneerer! You don't
know the depth of woman's feeling, the lofty
scorn of all deceit, the entire absence of mean
curiosity in the sex, or never, never would you
libel us so!" Ah, Delia! dear, dear Delia! It
is because I fancy I *do* know something about
you (not all, mind — no, no ; no man knows
that). Ah, my bride, my ringdove, my rose,
my poppet, — choose, in fact, whatever name
you like, — bulbul of my grove, fountain of my
desert, sunshine of my darkling life, and joy of
my dungeoned existence, it is because I *do* know
a little about you that I conclude to say nothing of that private closet, and keep my key in
my pocket. You take away that closet-key
then, and the house-key. You lock Delia in.
You keep her out of harm's way and gadding,
and so she never *can* be found out.

And yet by little strange accidents and coin-

cidents how we are being found out every day.
You remember that old story of the Abbé
Kakatoes, who told the company at supper one
night how the first confession he ever received
was — from a murderer, let us say. Presently
enters to supper the Marquis de Croquemitaine.
" Palsambleu, abbé ! " says the brilliant marquis, taking a pinch of snuff, "are you here ?
Gentlemen and ladies ! I was the abbé's first
penitent, and I made him a confession, which I
promise you astonished him."

To be sure how queerly things are found
out ! Here is an instance : Only the other day
I was writing in these Roundabout Papers about
a certain man, whom I facetiously called Baggs,
and who had abused me to my friends, who of
course told me. Shortly after that paper was
published another friend — Sacks let us call him
— scowls fiercely at me as I am sitting in perfect good-humor at the club, and passes on
without speaking. A cut. A quarrel. Sacks
thinks it is about him that I was writing :
whereas, upon my honor and conscience, I
never had him once in my mind, and was pointing my moral from quite another man. But
don't you see, by this wrath of the guilty-con-
scienced Sacks, that he had been abusing me
too ? He has owned himself guilty, never hav-

ing been accused. He has winced when nobody
thought of hitting him. I did but put the cap
out, and madly butting and chafing, behold my
friend rushes out to put his head into it! Never
mind, Sacks, you are found out; but I bear you
no malice, my man.

And yet to be found out, I know from my
own experience, must be painful and odious,
and cruelly mortifying to the inward vanity.
Suppose I am a poltroon, let us say. With
fierce moustache, loud talk, plentiful oaths, and
an immense stick, I keep up, nevertheless, a
character for courage. I swear fearfully at
cabmen and women ; brandish my bludgeon,
and perhaps knock down a little man or two
with it : brag of the images which I break at
the shooting - gallery, and pass amongst my
friends for a whiskery fire-eater, afraid of neither man nor dragon. Ah me! Suppose some
brisk little chap steps up and gives me a caning
in St. James's Street, with all the heads of my
friends looking out of all the club windows.
My reputation is gone. I frighten no man
more. My nose is pulled by whipper-snappers,
who jump up on a chair to reach it. I am
found out. And in the days of my triumphs,
when people were yet afraid of me, and were
taken in by my swagger, I always knew that I

was a lily-liver, and expected that I should be found out some day.

That certainty of being found out must haunt and depress many a bold braggadocio spirit. Let us say it is a clergyman, who can pump copious floods of tears out of his own eyes and those of his audience. He thinks to himself, "I am but a poor swindling, chattering rogue. My bills are unpaid. I have jilted several women whom I have promised to marry. I don't know whether I believe what I preach, and I know I have stolen the very sermon over which I have been sniveling. Have they found me out?" says he, as his head drops down on the cushion.

Then your writer, poet, historian, novelist, or what not? The *Beacon* says that "Jones's work is one of the first order." The *Lamp* declares that "Jones's tragedy surpasses every work since the days of Him of Avon." The *Comet* asserts that "J.'s 'Life of Goody Two-shoes' is a κτῆμα ἐς ἀεὶ, a noble and enduring monument to the fame of that admirable Eng-lishwoman," and so forth. But then Jones knows that he has lent the critic of the *Beacon* five pounds; that his publisher has a half-share in the *Lamp;* and that the *Comet* comes re-peatedly to dine with him. It is all very well.

Jones is immortal until he is found out; and then down comes the extinguisher, and the immortal is dead and buried. The idea (*dies iræ!*) of discovery must haunt many a man, and make him uneasy, as the trumpets are puffing in his triumph. Brown, who has a higher place than he deserves, cowers before Smith, who has found him out. What is the chorus of critics shouting "Bravo"? — a public clapping hands and flinging garlands? Brown knows that Smith has found him out. Puff, trumpets! Wave, banners! Huzza, boys, for the immortal Brown! "This is all very well," B. thinks (bowing the while, smiling, laying his hand to his heart); "but there stands Smith at the window: *he* has measured me; and some day the others will find me out too." It is a very curious sensation to sit by a man who has found you out, and who, as you know, has found you out; or, *vice versa*, to sit with a man whom *you* have found out. His talent? Bah! His virtue? We know a little story or two about his virtue, and he knows we know it. We are thinking over friend Robinson's antecedents, as we grin, bow, and talk; and we are both humbugs together. Robinson a good fellow, is he? You know how he behaved to Hicks? A good-natured man, is he? Pray do you remember that little story of Mrs. Robinson's black eye? How men have to work, to talk, to smile, to go to bed, and try and sleep, with this dread of being found out on their consciences! Bardolph, who has robbed a church, and Nym, who has taken a purse, go to their usual haunts, and smoke their pipes with their companions. Mr. Detective Bullseye appears, and says, " Oh, Bardolph! I want you about that there pyx business!" Mr. Bardolph knocks the ashes out of his pipe, puts out his hands to the little steel cuffs, and walks away quite meekly. He is found out. He must go. "Good-by, Doll Tearsheet! Good-by, Mrs. Quickly, ma'am!" The other gentlemen and ladies *de la société* look on and exchange mute adieux with the departing friends. And an assured time will come when the other gentlemen and ladies will be found out too.

What a wonderful and beautiful provision of nature it has been that, for the most part, our womankind are not endowed with the faculty of finding us out! *They* don't doubt, and probe, and weigh, and take your measure. Lay down this paper, my benevolent friend and reader, go into your drawing-room now, and utter a joke ever so old, and I wager sixpence the ladies there will all begin to laugh. Go to

Brown's house, and tell Mrs. Brown and the young ladies what you think of him, and see what a welcome you will get! In like manner, let him come to your house, and tell *your* good lady his candid opinion of you, and fancy how she will receive him! Would you have your wife and children know you exactly for what you are, and esteem you precisely at your worth? If so, my friend, you will live in a dreary house, and you will have but a chilly fireside. Do you suppose the people round it don't see your homely face as under a glamour, and, as it were, with a halo of love round it? You don't fancy you *are* as you seem to them? No such thing, my man. Put away that monstrous conceit, and be thankful that *they* have not found you out.

OGRES.

I DARE say the reader has remarked that the upright and independent vowel, which stands in the vowel-list between E and O, has formed the subject of the main part of these essays. How does that vowel feel this morning? —fresh, good-humored, and lively? The Roundabout lines, which fall from this pen, are

correspondingly brisk and cheerful. Has anything, on the contrary, disagreed with the
vowel? Has its rest been disturbed, or was
yesterday's dinner too good, or yesterday's wine
not good enough? Under such circumstances,
a darkling, misanthropic tinge, no doubt, is
cast upon the paper. The jokes, if attempted,
are elaborate and dreary. The bitter temper
breaks out. That sneering manner is adopted,
which you know, and which exhibits itself so
especially when the writer is speaking about
women. A moody carelessness comes over
him. He sees no good in anybody or thing:
and treats gentlemen, ladies, history, and things
in general, with a like gloomy flippancy. Agreed.
When the vowel in question is in that mood, if
you like airy gayety and tender gushing benevolence, if you want to be satisfied with yourself and the rest of your fellow-beings, I
recommend you, my dear creature, to go to
some other shop in Cornhill, or turn to some
other article. There are moods in the mind of
the vowel of which we are speaking, when it is
ill-conditioned and captious. Who always
keeps good health, and good humor? Do not
philosophers grumble? Are not sages sometimes out of temper? and do not angel-women
go off in tantrums? To-day my mood is dark.
I scowl as I dip my pen in the inkstand.

Here is the day come round — for everything here is done with the utmost regularity :
— intellectual labor, sixteen hours ; meals,
thirty-two minutes ; exercise, a hundred and
forty-eight minutes ; conversation with the
family, chiefly literary, and about the house-
keeping, one hour and four minutes ; sleep,
three hours and fifteen minutes (at the end of
the month, when the Magazine is complete, I
own I take eight minutes more) ; and the rest
for the toilet and the world. Well, I say, the
Roundabout Paper Day being come, and the
subject long since settled in my mind, an excellent subject, — a most telling, lively, and
popular subject, — I go to breakfast determined
to finish that meal in $9\frac{3}{4}$ minutes, as usual, and
then retire to my desk and work, when — oh,
provoking ! — here in the paper is the very
subject treated, on which I was going to write !
Yesterday another paper, which I saw, treated
it — and of course, as I need not tell you,
spoiled it. Last Saturday, another paper had
an article on the subject ; perhaps you may
guess what it was — but I won't tell you.
Only this is true, my favorite subject, which
was about to make the best paper we have had
for a long time : my bird, my game, that I was
going to shoot and serve up with such a delicate

sauce, has been found by other sportsmen ; and pop, pop, pop, a half dozen of guns have banged at it, mangled it, and brought it down.

"And can't you take some other text ?" say you. All this is mighty well. But if you have set your heart on a certain dish for dinner, be it cold boiled veal, or what you will, and they bring you turtle and venison, don't you feel disappointed ? During your walk you have been making up your mind that that cold meat, with moderation and a pickle, will be a very sufficient dinner : you have accustomed your thoughts to it ; and here, in place of it, is a turkey, surrounded by coarse sausages, or a reeking pigeon-pie, or a fulsome roast-pig. I have known many a good and kind man made furiously angry by such a *contretemps*. I have known him lose his temper, call his wife and servants names, and a whole household made miserable. If, then, as is notoriously the case, it is too dangerous to balk a man about his dinner, how much more about his article ? I came to my meal with an ogre-like appetite and gusto. Fee, faw, fum ! Wife, where is that tender little Princekin ? Have you trussed him, and did you stuff him nicely, and have you taken care to baste him and do him, not too brown, as I told you ? Quick ! I am hungry! I begin to whet my knife, to roll my eyes about, and roar and clap my huge chest like a gorilla; and then my poor Ogrina has to tell that the little princes have all run away, whilst she was in the kitchen, making the paste to bake them in! I pause in the description. I won't condescend to report the bad language, which you know must ensue, when an ogre, whose mind is ill-regulated, and whose habits of self-indulgence are notorious, finds himself disappointed of his greedy hopes. What treatment of his wife, what abuse and brutal behavior to his children, who, though ogrillons, are children! My dears, you may fancy, and need not ask my delicate pen to describe, the language and behavior of a vulgar, coarse, greedy, large man with an immense mouth and teeth, which are too frequently employed in the gobbling and crunching of raw man's meat.

And in this circuitous way, you see I have reached my present subject, which is, Ogres. You fancy they are dead or only fictitious characters — mythical representatives of strength, cruelty, stupidity, and lust for blood? Though they had seven-leagued boots, you remember all sorts of little whipping-snapping Tom Thumbs used to elude and outrun them. They were so stupid that they gave into the most shallow ambuscades and artifices : witness that well-known ogre, who, because Jack cut open the hasty-pudding, instantly ripped open his own stupid waistcoat and interior. They were cruel, brutal, disgusting, with their sharpened teeth, immense knives, and roaring voices ! but they always ended by being overcome by little Tom Thumbkins, or some other smart little champion.

Yes : they were conquered in the end there is no doubt. They plunged headlong (and uttering the most frightful bad language) into some pit where Jack came with his smart *couteau de chasse* and whipped their brutal heads off. They would be going to devour maidens,

> " But ever when it seemed
> Their need was at the sorest,
> A knight, in armor bright,
> Came riding through the forest."

And down, after a combat, would go the brutal persecutor, with a lance through his midriff. Yes, I say, this is very true and well. But you remember that round the ogre's cave the ground was covered, for hundreds and hundreds of yards, *with the bones of the victims* whom he had lured into the castle. Many knights and maids came to him and perished under his knife and teeth. Were dragons the same as

ogres? monsters dwelling in caverns, whence
they rushed, attired in plate armor, wielding
pikes and torches, and destroying stray pas-
sengers who passed by their lair? Monsters,
brutes, rapacious tyrants, ruffians as they were,
doubtless they ended by being overcome. But
before they were destroyed, they did a deal of
mischief. The bones round their caves were
countless. They had sent many brave souls to
Hades, before their own fled, howling out of
their rascal carcasses, to the same place of
gloom.

There is no greater mistake than to suppose
that fairies, champions, distressed damsels, and,
by consequence, ogres, have ceased to exist. It
may not be *ogreable* to them (pardon the horrible pleasantry, but as I am writing in the
solitude of my chamber, I am grinding my
teeth — yelling, roaring, and cursing — bran-
dishing my scissors and paper cutter, and, as it
were, have become an ogre). I say there is no
greater mistake than to suppose that ogres have
ceased to exist. We all *know* ogres. Their
caverns are round us, and about us. There are
the castles of several ogres within a mile of
the spot where I write. I think some of them
suspect I am an ogre myself. I am not: but
I know they are. I visit them. I don't mean

to say that they take a cold roast prince out of the cupboard, and have a cannibal feast before *me.* But I see the bones lying about the roads to their houses, and in the areas and gardens. Politeness, of course, prevents me from making any remarks; but I know them well enough. One of the ways to know 'em is to watch the scared looks of the ogres' wives and children. They lead an awful life. They are present at dreadful cruelties. In their excesses those ogres will stab about, and kill not only strangers who happen to call in and ask a night's lodgings, but they will outrage, murder, and chop up their own kin. We all know ogres, I say, and have been in their dens often. It is not necessary that ogres who ask you to dine should offer their guests the *peculiar dish* which they like. They cannot always get a Tom Thumb family. They eat mutton and beef too; and I dare say even go out to tea, and invite you to drink it. But I tell you there are numbers of them going about in the world. And now you have my word for it, and this little hint, it is quite curious what an interest society may be made to have for you, by your determining to find out the ogres you meet there.

What does the man mean? says Mrs. Downright, to whom a joke is a very grave thing. I

mean, madam, that in the company assembled
in your genteel drawing-room, who bow here
and there and smirk in white neck-cloths, you
receive men who elbow through life successfully
enough, but who are ogres in private : men
wicked, false, rapacious, flattering ; cruel hec-
tors at home, smiling courtiers abroad ; causing
wives, children, servants, parents, to tremble
before them, and smiling and bowing as they
bid strangers welcome into their castles. I say,
there are men who have crunched the bones of
victim after victim ; in whose closets lie skel-
etons picked frightfully clean. When these
ogres come out into the world, you don't suppose they show their knives, and their great
teeth ? A neat simple white neck - cloth, a
merry rather obsequious manner, a cadaver-
ous look, perhaps, now and again, and a rather
dreadful grin : but I know ogres very consid-
erably respected : and when you hint to such
and such a man, "My dear sir, Mr. Sharpus,
whom you appear to like, is, I assure you, a
most dreadful cannibal," the gentleman cries,
"Oh, psha, nonsense ! Dare say not so black
as he is painted. Dare say not worse than his
neighbors." We condone everything in this
country — private treason, falsehood, flattery,
cruelty at home, roguery, and double-dealing.

What! Do you mean to say in your acquaintance you don't know ogres guilty of countless crimes of fraud and force, and that knowing them you don't shake hands with them; dine with them at your table; and meet them at their own? Depend upon it, in the time when there were real live ogres in real caverns or castles, gobbling up real knights and virgins, when they went into the world — the neighboring market-town, let us say, or earl's castle — though their nature and reputation were pretty well known, their notorious foibles were never alluded to. You would say, "What, Blunderbore, my boy! How do you do? How well and fresh you look! What's the receipt you have for keeping so young and rosy?" And your wife would softly ask after Mrs. Blunderbore and the dear children. Or it would be, "My dear Humguffin! try that pork. It is home-bred, home-fed, and, I promise you, tender. Tell me if you think it is as good as yours? John, a glass of Burgundy to Colonel Humguffin!" You don't suppose there would be any unpleasant allusions to disagreeable home-reports regarding Humguffin's manner of furnishing his larder? I say we all of us know ogres. We shake hands and dine with ogres. And if inconvenient moralists tell us we are cowards for our pains, we turn round with a *tu quoque*, or say that we don't meddle with other folks' affairs ; that people are much less black than they are painted, and so on. What ! Won't half the country go to Ogreham Castle ? Won't some of the clergy say grace at dinner ? Won't the mothers bring their daughters to dance with the young Rawheads ? And if Lady Ogreham happens to die — I won't say to go the way of all flesh, that is too revolting — I say if Ogreham is a widower, do you aver, on your conscience and honor, that mothers will not be found to offer their young girls to supply the lamented lady's place ? How stale this misanthropy is ! Something must have disagreed with this cynic. Yes, my good woman. I dare say you would like to call another subject. Yes, my fine fellow ; ogre at home, supple as a dancing-master abroad, and shaking in thy pumps, and wearing a horrible grin of sham gayety to conceal thy terror, lest I should point thee out : — thou art prosperous and honored, art thou ? I say thou hast been a tyrant and a robber. Thou hast plundered the poor. Thou hast bullied the weak. Thou hast laid violent hands on the goods of the innocent and confiding. Thou hast made a prey of the meek and gentle who asked for thy protection. Thou hast been hard to thy kinsfolk, and cruel to thy family. Go, monster! Ah, when shall little Jack come and drill daylight through thy wicked cannibal carcass? I see the ogre pass on, bowing right and left to the company; and he gives a dreadful sidelong glance of suspicion as he is talking to my lord bishop in the corner there.

Ogres in our days need not be giants at all. In former times, and in children's books, where it is necessary to paint your moral in such large letters that there can be no mistake about it, ogres are made with that enormous mouth and *ratelier* which you know of, and with which they can swallow down a baby, almost without using that great knife which they always carry. They are too cunning nowadays. They go about in society, slim, small, quietly dressed, and showing no especially great appetite. In my own young days there used to be play ogres — men who would devour a young fellow in one sitting, and leave him without a bit of flesh on his bones. They were quiet, gentleman-like-looking people. They got the young fellow into their cave. Champagne, *pâté-de-foie-gras*, and numberless good things were handed about; and then, having eaten, the young man was devoured in his turn. I believe these card and

dice ogres have died away almost as entirely as
the hasty-pudding giants whom Tom Thumb
overcame. Now, there are ogres in City courts
who lure you into their dens. About our
Cornish mines I am told there are many most
plausible ogres, who tempt you into their caverns and pick your bones there. In a certain
newspaper there used to be lately a whole col-
umn of advertisements from ogres who would
put on the most plausible, nay, piteous appearance, in order to inveigle their victims. You
would read, " A tradesman, established for
seventy years in the City, and known, and much
respected by Messrs. N. M. Rothschild and
Baring Brothers, has pressing need for three
pounds until next Saturday. He can give
security for half a million, and forty thousand
pounds will be given for the use of the loan,"
and so on ; or, " An influential body of capital-
ists are about to establish a company, of which
the business will be enormous and the profits
proportionately prodigious. They will require
a SECRETARY, of good address and appearance,
at a salary of two thousand pounds per annum.
He need not be able to write, but address and
manners are absolutely necessary. As a mark
of confidence in the company, he will have to
deposit," etc. ; or, " A young widow (of pleas-

ing manners and appearance) who has a pressing
necessity for four pounds ten for three weeks,
offers her Erard's grand piano, valued at three
hundred guineas; a diamond cross of eight
hundred pounds; and board and lodging in her
elegant villa near Banbury Cross, with the best
references and society, in return for the loan."
I suspect these people are ogres. There are
ogres and ogres. Polyphemus was a great,
tall, one-eyed, notorious ogre, fetching his victims out of a hole, and gobbling them one after
another. There could be no mistake about
him. But so were the Sirens ogres — pretty
blue-eyed things, peeping at you coaxingly from
out of the water, and singing their melodious
wheedles. And the bones round their caves
were more numerous than the ribs, skulls, and
thigh-bones round the cavern of hulking Poly-
pheme.

To the castle-gates of some of these monsters
up rides the dapper champion of the pen; puffs
boldly upon the horn which hangs by the chain;
enters the hall resolutely, and challenges the
big tyrant sulking within. We defy him to
combat, the enormous roaring ruffian! We
gave him a meeting on the green plain before
his castle. Green? No wonder it should be
green: it is manured with human bones. After

a few graceful wheels and curvets, we take our ground. We stoop over our saddle. 'T is but to kiss the locket of our lady-love's hair. And now the visor is up : the lance is in rest (Gillott's iron is the point for me). A touch of the spur in the gallant sides of Pegasus, and we gallop at the great brute.

"Cut off his ugly head, Flibbertygibbet, my squire ! " And who are these who pour out of the castle ? the imprisoned maidens, the maltreated widows, the poor old hoary grandfathers, who have been locked up in the dungeons these scores and scores of years, writhing under the tyranny of that ruffian! Ah, ye knights of the pen ! May honor be your shield, and truth tip your lances ! Be gentle to all gentle people. Be modest to women. Be tender to children. And as for the Ogre Humbug, out sword, and have at him.

NIL NISI BONUM.

ALMOST the last words which Sir Walter spoke to Lockhart, his biographer, were, "Be a good man, my dear ! " and with the last flicker of breath on his dying lips, he sighed a farewell to his family, and passed away blessing them.

Two men, famous, admired, beloved, have just left us, the Goldsmith and the Gibbon of our time.[1] Ere a few weeks are over, many a critic's pen will be at work, reviewing their lives, and passing judgment on their works. This is no review, or history, or criticism : only a word in testimony of respect and regard from a man of letters, who owes to his own professional labor the honor of becoming acquainted with these two eminent literary men. One was the first ambassador whom the New World of Letters sent to the Old. He was born almost with the republic ; the *pater patriæ* had laid his hand on the child's head. He bore Washington's name : he came amongst us bringing the kindest sympathy, the most artless, smiling good-will. His new country (which some people here might be disposed to regard rather superciliously) could send us, as he showed in his own person, a gentleman, who, though himself born in no very high sphere, was most finished, polished, easy, witty, quiet ; and socially, the equal of the most refined Europeans. If Irving's welcome in England was a kind one, was it not also gratefully remembered ? If he ate our salt, did he not pay us with a thank-

---

[1] Washington Irving died, November 28, 1859; Lord Macaulay died, December 28, 1859.

ful heart? Who can calculate the amount of
friendliness and good feeling for our country
which this writer's generous and untiring regard
for us disseminated in his own? His books
are read by millions [1] of his countrymen, whom
he has taught to love England, and why to love
her. It would have been easy to speak otherwise than he did: to inflame national rancors,
which, at the time when he first became known
as a public writer, war had just renewed: to
cry down the old civilization at the expense of
the new: to point out our faults, arrogance,
short-comings, and give the republic to infer
how much she was the parent state's superior.
There are writers enough in the United States,
honest and otherwise, who preach that kind of
doctrine. But the good Irving, the peaceful,
the friendly, had no place for bitterness in his
heart, and no scheme but kindness. Received
in England with extraordinary tenderness and
friendship (Scott, Southey, Byron, a hundred
others have borne witness to their liking for
him), he was a messenger of good-will and
peace between his country and ours. "See,
friends!" he seems to say, "these English are
not so wicked, rapacious, callous, proud, as you

[1] See his *Life* in the most remarkable *Dictionary of Authors*, published lately at Philadelphia, by Mr. Allibone.

have been taught to believe them. I went amongst them a humble man ; won my way by my pen ; and, when known, found every hand held out to me with kindliness and welcome. Scott is a great man, you acknowledge. Did not Scott's King of England give a gold medal to him, and another to me, your countryman, and a stranger ? "

Tradition in the United States still fondly retains the history of the feasts and rejoicings which awaited Irving on his return to his native country from Europe. He had a national welcome; he stammered in his speeches, hid himself in confusion, and the people loved him all the better. He had worthily represented America in Europe. In that young community a man who brings home with him abundant European testimonials is still treated with respect (I have found American writers, of world-wide reputation, strangely solicitous about the opinions of quite obscure British critics, and elated or depressed by their judgments); and Irving went home medaled by the King, diplomatized by the University, crowned and honored and admired. He had not in any way intrigued for his honors, he had fairly won them ; and, in Irving's instance, as in others, the old country was glad and eager to pay them.

In America the love and regard for Irving was a national sentiment. Party wars are perpetually raging there, and are carried on by the press with a rancor and fierceness against individuals which exceed British, almost Irish, virulence. It seemed to me, during a year's travel in the country, as if no one ever aimed a blow at Irving. All men held their hand from that harmless, friendly peacemaker. I had the good fortune to see him at New York, Philadelphia, Baltimore, and Washington,[1] and remarked how in every place he was honored and welcome. Every large city has its "Irving House." The country takes pride in the fame of its men of letters. The gate of his own charming little domain on the beautiful Hudson River was forever swinging before visitors who came to him. He shut out no one.[2] I had

---

[1] At Washington, Mr. Irving came to a lecture given by the writer, which Mr. Filmore and General Pierce, the President and President Elect, were also kind enough to attend together. "Two Kings of Brentford smelling at one rose," says Irving, looking up with his good-humored smile.

[2] Mr. Irving described to me, with that humor and good-humor which he always kept, how, amongst other visitors, a member of the British press who had carried his distinguished pen to America (where he employed it in vilifying his own country) came to Sunnyside, introduced himself to Irving, partook of his wine and luncheon, and in two days described Mr. Irving, his house, his nieces, his meal, and his

seen many pictures of his house, and read descriptions of it, in both of which it was treated with a not unusual American exaggeration. It was but a pretty little cabin of a place; the gentleman of the press who took notes of the place, whilst his kind old host was sleeping, might have visited the whole house in a couple of minutes.

And how came it that this house was so small, when Mr. Irving's books were sold by hundreds of thousands, nay, millions, when his profits were known to be large, and the habits of life of the good old bachelor were notoriously modest and simple? He had loved once in his life. The lady he loved died; and he, whom all the world loved, never sought to replace her. I can't say how much the thought of that fidelity has touched me. Does not the very cheerfulness of his after life add to the pathos of that untold story? To grieve always was not in his nature; or, when he had his sorrow, to bring all the world in to condole with him and bemoan it. Deep and quiet he lays the love of his heart, and buries it; and grass and

manner of dozing afterwards, in a New York paper. On another occasion, Irving said, laughing, "Two persons came to me, and one held me in conversation whilst the other miscreant took my portrait!"

flowers grow over the scarred ground in due time.

Irving had such a small house and such narrow rooms, because there was a great number of people to occupy them. He could only afford to keep one old horse (which, lazy and aged as it was, managed once or twice to run away with that careless old horseman). He could only afford to give plain sherry to that amiable British paragraph-monger from New York, who saw the patriarch asleep over his modest, blameless cup, and fetched the public into his private chamber to look at him. Irving could only live very modestly, because the wifeless, childless man had a number of children to whom he was as a father. He had as many as nine nieces, I am told — I saw two of these ladies at his house — with all of whom the dear old man had shared the produce of his labor and genius.

"*Be a good man, my dear.*" One can't but think of these last words of the veteran Chief of Letters, who had tasted and tested the value of worldly success, admiration, prosperity. Was Irving not good, and, of his works, was not his life the best part? In his family, gentle, generous, good - humored, affectionate, self-denying : in society, a delightful example of complete gentlemanhood; quite unspoiled by prosperity; never obsequious to the great (or, worse still, to the base and mean, as some public men are forced to be in his and other countries); eager to acknowledge every contemporary's merit; always kind and affable to the young members of his calling; in his professional bargains and mercantile dealings delicately honest and grateful; one of the most charming masters of our lighter language; the constant friend to us and our nation; to men of letters doubly dear, not for his wit and genius merely, but as an exemplar of goodness, probity, and pure life: I don't know what sort of testimonial will be raised to him in his own country, where generous and enthusiastic acknowledgment of American merit is never wanting; but Irving was in our service as well as theirs; and as they have placed a stone at Greenwich yonder in memory of that gallant young Bellot, who shared the perils and fate of some of our Arctic seamen, I would like to hear of some memorial raised by English writers and friends of letters in affectionate remembrance of the dear and good Washington Irving.

As for the other writer, whose departure many friends, some few most dearly-loved relatives, and multitudes of admiring readers deplore, our republic has already decreed his statue, and he must have known that he had earned this posthumous honor. He is not a poet and man of letters merely, but citizen, statesman, a great British worthy. Almost from the first moment when he appears, amongst boys, amongst college students, amongst men, he is marked, and takes rank as a great Englishman. All sorts of successes are easy to him : as a lad he goes down into the arena with others, and wins all the prizes to which he has a mind. A place in the senate is straightway offered to the young man. He takes his seat there ; he speaks, when so minded, without party anger or intrigue, but not without party faith and a sort of heroic enthusiasm for his cause. Still he is poet and philosopher even more than orator. That he may have leisure and means to pursue his darling studies, he absents himself for a while, and accepts a richly-remunerative post in the East. As learned a man may live in a cottage or a college common-room ; but it always seemed to me that ample means and recognized rank were Macaulay's as of right. Years ago there was a wretched outcry raised because Mr. Macaulay dated a letter from Windsor Castle, where he was staying. Immortal gods ! Was this man not a fit guest

for any palace in the world, or a fit companion
for any man or woman in it ?   I dare say, after
Austerlitz, the old K. K. court officials and
footmen sneered at Napoleon for dating from
Schönbrunn.   But that miserable "Windsor
Castle" outcry is an echo out of fast-retreating
old-world remembrances.   The place of such a
natural chief was amongst the first of the land ;
and that country is best, according to our British
notion at least, where the man of eminence has
the best chance of investing his genius and intellect.

If a company of giants were got together,
very likely one or two of the mere six-feet-six
people might be angry at the incontestable superiority of the very tallest of the party ; and
so I have heard some London wits, rather pee-
vish at Macaulay's superiority, complain that
he occupied too much of the talk, and so forth.
Now that wonderful tongue is to speak no more,
will not many a man grieve that he no longer
has the chance to listen ?   To remember the
talk is to wonder : to think not only of the
treasures he had in his memory, but of the
trifles he had stored there, and could produce
with equal readiness.   Almost on the last day
I had the fortune to see him, a conversation
happened suddenly to spring up about senior

wranglers, and what they had done in after life. To the almost terror of the persons present, Macaulay began with the senior wrangler of 1801-2-3-4, and so on, giving the name of each, and relating his subsequent career and rise. Every man who has known him has his story regarding that astonishing memory. It may be that he was not ill pleased that you should recognize it ; but to those prodigious intellectual feats, which were so easy to him, who would grudge his tribute of homage ? His talk was, in a word, admirable, and we admired it.

Of the notices which have appeared regarding Lord Macaulay, up to the day when the present lines are written (the 9th of January), the reader should not deny himself the pleasure of looking especially at two. It is a good sign of the times when such articles as these (I mean the articles in *The Times* and *Saturday Review*) appear in our public prints about our public men. They educate us, as it were, to admire rightly. An uninstructed person in a museum or at a concert may pass by without recognizing a picture or a passage of music, which the connoisseur by his side may show him is a masterpiece of harmony, or a wonder of artistic skill. After reading these papers you like and respect

more the person you have admired so much
already.   And so with regard to Macaulay's
style there may be faults of course — what
critic can't point them out ?   But for the nonce
we are not talking about faults : we want to
say *nil nisi bonum.*   Well — take at hazard any
three pages of the " Essays " or " History ; " —
and, glimmering below the stream of the nar-
rative, as it were, you, an average reader, see
one, two, three, a half-score of allusions to other
historic facts, characters, literature, poetry,
with which you are acquainted.   Why is this
epithet used ?   Whence is that simile drawn ?
How does he manage, in two or three words, to
paint an individual, or to indicate a landscape ?
Your neighbor, who has *his* reading, and his
little stock of literature stowed away in his
mind, shall detect more points, allusions, happy
touches, indicating not only the prodigious
memory and vast learning of this master, but
the wonderful industry, the honest, humble
previous toil of this great scholar.   He reads
twenty books to write a sentence ; he travels a
hundred miles to make a line of description.

Many Londoners — not all — have seen the
British Museum Library.   I speak *à cœur ouvert*
and pray the kindly reader to bear with me.   I
have seen all sorts of domes of Peters and

Pauls, Sophia, Pantheon, — what not? — and
have been struck by none of them so much as
by that catholic dome in Bloomsbury, under
which our million volumes are housed. What
peace, what love, what truth, what beauty, what
happiness for all, what generous kindness for
you and me, are here spread out! It seems to
me one cannot sit down in that place without a
heart full of grateful reverence. I own to have
said my grace at the table, and to have thanked
Heaven for this my English birthright, freely to
partake of these bountiful books, and to speak
the truth I find there. Under the dome which
held Macaulay's brain, and from which his
solemn eyes looked out on the world but a
fortnight since, what a vast, brilliant, and
wonderful store of learning was ranged! what
strange lore would he not fetch for you at your
bidding! A volume of law, or history, a book
of poetry familiar or forgotten (except by himself who forgot nothing), a novel ever so old,
and he had it at hand. I spoke to him once
about "Clarissa." "Not read 'Clarissa!'" he
cried out. "If you have once thoroughly entered on 'Clarissa' and are infected by it, you
can't leave it. When I was in India I passed
one hot season at the hills, and there were the
Governor-General, and the Secretary of Gov-

ernment, and the Commander - in - Chief, and
their wives. I had 'Clarissa' with me: and, as
soon as they began to read, the whole station
was in a passion of excitement about Miss Har-
lowe and her misfortunes, and her scoundrelly
Lovelace! The Governor's wife seized the
book, and the Secretary waited for it, and the
Chief Justice could not read it for tears!" He
acted the whole scene: he paced up and down
the " Athenæum " library: I dare say he could
have spoken pages of the book — of that book,
and of what countless piles of others!

In this little paper let us keep to the text of
nil nisi bonum. One paper I have read regarding Lord Macaulay says " he had no heart."
Why, a man's books may not always speak the
truth, but they speak his mind in spite of himself: and it seems to me this man's heart is
beating through every page he penned. He is
always in a storm of revolt and indignation
against wrong, craft, tyranny. How he cheers
heroic resistance ; how he backs and applauds
freedom struggling for its own ; how he hates
scoundrels, ever so victorious and successful ;
how he recognizes genius, though selfish villains
possess it! The critic who says Macaulay had
no heart might say that Johnson had none :
and two men more generous, and more loving,

and more hating, and more partial, and more noble, do not live in our history. Those who knew Lord Macaulay knew how admirably tender and generous,[1] and affectionate he was. It was not his business to bring his family before the theatre foot-lights, and call for bouquets from the gallery as he wept over them.

If any young man of letters reads this little sermon — and to him, indeed, it is addressed — I would say to him, "Bear Scott's words in your mind, and '*be good, my dear.*'" Here are two literary men gone to their account, and, *laus Deo*, as far as we know, it is fair, and open, and clean. Here is no need of apologies for shortcomings, or explanations of vices which would have been virtues but for unavoidable, etc. Here are two examples of men most differently gifted : each pursuing his calling ; each speaking his truth as God bade him ; each honest in his life ; just and irreproachable in his dealings ; dear to his friends ; honored by his country ; beloved at his fireside. It has been the fortunate lot of both to give incalculable happiness and delight to the world, which thanks them in return with an immense kindliness, respect, af-

---

[1] Since the above was written, I have been informed that it has been found, on examining Lord Macaulay's papers, that he was in the habit of giving away *more than a fourth part* of his annual income.

fection. It may not be our chance, brother scribe, to be endowed with such merit, or rewarded with such fame. But the rewards of these men are rewards paid to *our service*. We may not win the *bâton* or epaulets ; but God give us strength to guard the honor of the flag !

DE FINIBUS.

WHEN Swift was in love with Stella, and despatching her a letter from London thrice a month by the Irish packet, you remember how he would begin letter No. XXIII., we will say, on the very day when XXII. had been sent away, stealing out of the coffee-house or the assembly so as to be able to prattle with his dear ; " never letting go her kind hand, as it were," as some commentator or other has said in speaking of the Dean and his amour. When Mr. Johnson, walking to Dodsley's and touching the posts in Pall Mall as he walked, forgot to pat the head of one of them, he went back and imposed his hands on it, — impelled I know not by what superstition. I have this I hope not dangerous mania too. As soon as a piece of work is out of hand, and before going to sleep, I like to begin another : it may be to write only half a dozen lines! but that is something towards Number the Next. The printer's boy has not yet reached Green Arbor Court with the copy. Those people who were alive half an hour since, Pendennis, Clive Newcome, and (what do you call him? what was the name of the last hero? I remember now!) Philip Firmin, have hardly drunk their glass of wine, and the mammas have only this minute got the children's cloaks on, and have been bowed out of my premises —and here I come back to the study again: *tamen usque recurro.* How lonely it looks now all these people are gone! My dear good friends, some folks are utterly tired of you, and say, " What a poverty of friends the man has! He is always asking us to meet those Pendennises, Newcomes, and so forth. Why does he not introduce us to some new characters.? Why is he not thrilling like Twostars, learned and profound like Threestars, exquisitely humorous and human like Fourstars? Why, finally, is he not somebody else?" My good people, it is not only impossible to please you all, but it is absurd to try it. The dish which one man devours, another dislikes. Is the dinner of to-day not to your taste? Let us hope to-morrow's entertainment will be more agreeable. . . . . I resume my original subject. What an odd, pleasant, humorous, melancholy feeling it is to sit in the study, alone and quiet, now all these people are gone who have been boarding and lodging with me for twenty months ! They have interrupted my rest : they have plagued me at all sorts of minutes : they have thrust themselves upon me when I was ill, or wished to be idle, and I have growled out a " Be hanged to you, can't you leave me alone now?" Once or twice they have prevented my going out to dinner. Many and many a time they have ·prevented my coming home, because I knew they were there waiting in the study, and a plague take them ! and I have left home and family, and gone to dine at the Club, and told nobody where I went. They have bored me, those people. They have plagued me at all sorts of uncomfortable hours. They have made such a disturbance in my mind and house, that sometimes I have hardly known what was going on in my family, and scarcely have heard what my neighbor said to me. They are gone at last ; and you would expect me to be at ease ? Far from it. I should almost be glad if Woolcomb would walk in and talk to me ; or Twysden reappear, take his place in that chair opposite me, and begin one of his tremendous stories.

Madmen, you know, see visions, hold conver-

sations with, even draw the likeness of people
invisible to you and me. Is this making of
people out of fancy madness? and are novel-
writers at all entitled to strait-waistcoats? I
often forget people's names in life; and in my
own stories contritely own that I make dreadful blunders regarding them; but I declare,
my dear sir, with respect to the personages introduced into your humble servant's fables, I
know the people utterly — I know the sound of
their voices. A gentleman came in to see me
the other day, who was so like the picture of
Philip Firmin in Mr. Walker's charming drawings in the *Cornhill Magazine* that he was
quite a curiosity to me. The same eyes, beard,
shoulders, just as you have seen them from
month to month. Well, he is not like the
Philip Firmin in my mind. Asleep, asleep in
the grave, lies the bold, the generous, the reck-
less, the tender-hearted creature whom I have
made to pass through those adventures which
have just been brought to an end. It is years
since I heard the laughter ringing, or saw the
bright blue eyes. When I knew him both were
young. I become young as I think of him.
And this morning he was alive again in this
room, ready to laugh, to fight, to weep. As I
write, do you know, it is the gray of evening;

the house is quiet ; everybody is out ; the room
is getting a little dark, and I look rather wistfully up from the paper with perhaps ever so
much little fancy that HE MAY COME IN.
—No ? No movement. No gray shade, growing more palpable, out of which at last look the
well-known eyes. No, the printer came and
took him away with the last page of the proofs.
And with the printer's boy did the whole *cor-
tège* of ghosts flit away, invisible ? Ha ! stay !
what is this ? Angels and ministers of grace !
The door opens, and a dark form — enters, bearing a black — a black suit of clothes. It is
John. He says it is time to dress for dinner.

. . . .

Every man who has had his German tutor,
and has been coached through the famous
"Faust" of Goethe (thou wert my instructor,
good old Weissenborn, and these eyes beheld
the great master himself in dear little Weimar
town !) has read those charming verses which
are prefixed to the drama, in which the poet
reverts to the time when his work was first
composed, and recalls the friends now departed,
who once listened to his song. The dear
shadows rise up around him, he says ; he lives
in the past again. It is to-day which appears
vague and visionary. We humbler writers can-

not create Fausts, or raise up monumental works that shall endure for all ages ; but our books are diaries, in which our own feelings must of necessity be set down. As we look to the page written last month, or ten years ago, we remember the day and its events ; the child ill, mayhap, in the adjoining room, and the doubts and fears which racked the brain as it still pursued its work ; the dear old friend who read the commencement of the tale, and whose gentle hand shall be laid in ours no more. I own for my part that, in reading pages which this hand penned formerly, I often lose sight of the text under my eyes. It is not the words I see, but that past day ; that by-gone page of life's history ; that tragedy, comedy it may be, which our little home company was enacting ; that merry - making which we shared ; that funeral which we followed ; that bitter, bitter grief which we buried.

And, such being the state of my mind, I pray gentle readers to deal kindly with their humble servant's manifold shortcomings, blunders, and slips of memory. As sure as I read a page of my own composition, I find a fault or two, half a dozen. Jones is called Brown. Brown, who is dead, is brought to life. Aghast, and months after the number was printed, I saw that I had

called Philip Firmin, Clive Newcome. Now
Clive Newcome is the hero of another story by
the reader's most obedient writer. The two
men are as different, in my mind's eye, as — as
Lord Palmerston and Mr. Disraeli, let us say.
But there is that blunder at page 990, line 76,
volume 84 of the *Cornhill Magazine*, and it is
past mending ; and I wish in my life I had
made no worse blunders or errors than that
which is hereby acknowledged.

Another Finis written. Another mile-stone
passed on this journey from birth to the next
world ! Sure it is a subject for solemn cogita-
tion. Shall we continue this story-telling business and be voluble to the end of our age ?
Will it not be presently time, O prattler, to
hold your tongue, and let younger people
speak ? I have a friend, a painter, who, like
other persons who shall be nameless, is growing
old. He has never painted with such laborious
finish as his works now show. This master is
still the most humble and diligent of scholars.
Of Art, his mistress, he is always an eager,
reverent pupil. In his calling, in yours, in
mine, industry and humility will help and comfort us. A word with you. In a pretty large
experience I have not found the men who write
books superior in wit or learning to those who

don't write at all. In regard of mere information, non-writers must often be superior to
writers. You don't expect a lawyer in full
practice to be conversant with all kinds of literature ; he is too busy with his law ; and so a
writer is commonly too busy with his own books
to be able to bestow attention on the works of
other people. After a day's work (in which I
have been depicting, let us say, the agonies of
Louisa on parting with the Captain, or the
atrocious behavior of the wicked Marquis to
Lady Emily) I march to the Club, proposing to
improve my mind and keep myself "posted
up," as the Americans phrase it, with the literature of the day. And what happens ? Given
a walk after luncheon, a pleasing book, and a
most comfortable arm-chair by the fire, and
you know the rest. A doze ensues. Pleasing
book drops suddenly, is picked up once with an
air of some confusion, is laid presently softly
in lap : head falls on comfortable arm-chair
cushion : eyes close : soft nasal music is heard.
Am I telling Club secrets ? Of afternoons,
after lunch, I say, scores of sensible fogies have
a doze. Perhaps I have fallen asleep over
that very book to which "Finis" has just been
written. "And if the writer sleeps, what happens to the readers ?" says Jones, coming down

upon me with his lightning wit. What? You
did sleep over it ? And a very good thing too.
These eyes have more than once seen a friend
dozing over pages which this hand has written.
There is a vignette somewhere in one of my
books of a friend so caught napping with " Pendennis," or the "Newcomes," in his lap ; and
if a writer can give you a sweet soothing, harmless sleep, has he not done you a kindness ? So
is the author who excites and interests you
worthy of your thanks and benedictions. I am
troubled with fever and ague, that seizes me
at odd intervals and prostrates me for a day.
There is cold fit, for which, I am thankful to
say, hot brandy-and-water is prescribed, and
this induces hot fit, and so on. In one or two
of these fits I have read novels with the most
fearful contentment of mind. Once, on the
Mississippi, it was my dearly beloved " Jacob
Faithful : " once at Frankfort O. M., the delightful " Vingt Ans Après " of Monsieur
Dumas : once at Tunbridge Wells, the thrilling " Woman in White : " and these books gave
me amusement from morning till sunset. I
remember those ague fits with a great deal of
pleasure and gratitude. Think of a whole day
in bed, and a good novel for a companion ! No
cares : no remorse about idleness : no visitors ;

and the Woman in White or the Chevalier
d'Artagnan to tell me stories from dawn to
night ! "Please, ma'am, my master's compliments, and can he have the third volume ?"
(This message was sent to an astonished friend
and neighbor who lent me, volume by volume,
the *W. in W.*) How do you like your novels ?
I like mine strong, "hot with," and no mistake :
no love-making : no observations about society :
little dialogue, except where the characters are
bullying each other : plenty of fighting : and a
villain in the cupboard, who is to suffer tor-
tures just before Finis. I don't like your melancholy Finis. I never read the history of a
consumptive heroine twice. If I might give a
short hint to an impartial writer (as the *Exam-
iner* used to say in old days), it would be to act,
not á la mode le pays de Pole (I think that was
the phraseology), but *always* to give quarter.
In the story of Philip, just come to an end, I
have the permission of the author to state that
he was going to drown the two villains of the
piece — a certain Doctor F—— and a certain
Mr. T. H—— on board the "President," or
some other tragic ship — but you see I relented.
I pictured to myself Firmin's ghastly face amid
the crowd of shuddering people on that reeling
deck in the lonely ocean, and thought, "Thou

ghastly lying wretch, thou shalt not be drowned :
thou shalt have a fever only ; a knowledge of
thy danger ; and a chance — ever so small a
chance — of repentance." I wonder whether
he *did* repent when he found himself in the
yellow-fever, in Virginia ? The probability is,
he fancied that his son had injured him very
much, and forgave him on his death-bed. Do
you imagine there is a great deal of genuine
right-down remorse in the world ? Don't people rather find excuses which make their minds
easy ; endeavor to prove to themselves that
they have been lamentably belied and misun-
derstood ; and try and forgive the persecutors
who *will* present that bill when it is due ; and
not bear malice against the cruel ruffian who
takes them to the police-office for stealing the
spoons ? Years ago I had a quarrel with a
certain well-known person (I believed a statement regarding him which his friends imparted
to me, and which turned out to be quite incor-
rect). To his dying day that quarrel was never
quite made up. I said to his brother, " Why is
your brother's soul still dark against me ? It
is I who ought to be angry and unforgiving :
for I was in the wrong." In the region which
they now inhabit (for Finis has been set to the
volumes of the lives of both here below) if they

take any cognizance of our squabbles, and tittle-tattles, and gossips on earth here, I hope they admit that my little error was not of a nature unpardonable. If you have never committed a worse, my good sir, surely the score against you will not be heavy. Ha, *dilectissimi fratres!* It is in regard of sins *not* found out that we may say or sing (in an undertone, in a most penitent and lugubrious minor key) *Miserere nobis miseris peccatoribus.*

Among the sins of commission which novel-writers not seldom perpetrate, is the sin of grandiloquence, or tall-talking, against which, for my part, I will offer up a special *libera me.* This is the sin of schoolmasters, governesses, critics, sermoners, and instructors of young or old people. Nay (for I am making a clean breast, and liberating my soul), perhaps of all the novel-spinners now extant, the present speaker is the most addicted to preaching. Does he not stop perpetually in his story and begin to preach to you? When he ought to be engaged with business, is he not forever taking the Muse by the sleeve, and plaguing her with some of his cynical sermons? I cry *peccavi* loudly and heartily. I tell you I would like to be able to write a story which should show no egotism whatever — in which there should be no reflections, no cynicism, no vulgarity (and so forth), but an incident in every other page, a villain, a battle, a mystery in every chapter. I should like to be able to feed a reader so spicily as to leave him hungering and thirsting for more at the end of every monthly meal.

Alexandre Dumas describes himself, when inventing the plan of a work, as lying silent on his back for two whole days on the deck of a yacht in a Mediterranean port. At the end of the two days he arose and called for dinner. In those two days he had built his plot. He had moulded a mighty clay, to be cast presently in perennial brass. The chapters, the characters, the incidents, the combinations were all arranged in the artist's brain ere he set a pen to paper. My Pegasus won't fly, so as to let me survey the field below me. He has no wings, he is blind of one eye certainly, he is restive, stubborn, slow; crops a hedge when he ought to be galloping, or gallops when he ought to be quiet. He never will show off when I want him. Sometimes he goes at a pace which surprises me. Sometimes, when I most wish him to make the running, the brute turns restive, and I am obliged to let him take his own time. I wonder do other novel-writers

experience this fatalism? They *must* go a
certain way, in spite of themselves. I have
been surprised at the observations made by
some of my characters. It seems as if an
occult Power was moving the pen. The personage does or says something, and I ask, how
the dickens did he come to think of that?
Every man has remarked in dreams, the vast
dramatic power which is sometimes evinced ; I
won't say the surprising power, for nothing does
surprise you in dreams. But those strange
characters you meet make instant observations
of which you never can have thought previously.
In like manner, the imagination foretells things.
We spake anon of the inflated style of some
writers. What also if there is an *afflated* style,
— when a writer is like a Pythoness on her
oracle tripod, and mighty words, words which
he cannot help, come blowing, and bellowing,
and whistling, and moaning through the speaking pipes of his bodily organ? I have told you
it was a very queer shock to me the other day
when, with a letter of introduction in his hand,
the artist's (not my) Philip Firmin walked into
this room, and sat down in the chair opposite.
In the novel of " Pendennis," written ten years
ago, there is an account of a certain Costigan,
whom I had invented (as I suppose authors in-

vent their personages out of scraps, heel-taps, odds and ends of characters). I was smoking in a tavern parlor one night—and this Costigan came into the room alive—the very man :—the most remarkable resemblance of the printed sketches of the man, of the rude drawings in which I had depicted him. He had the same little coat, the same battered hat, cocked on one eye, the same twinkle in that eye. "Sir," said I, knowing him to be an old friend whom I had met in unknown regions, "sir," I said, "may I offer you a glass of brandy-and-water ? " " *Bedad, ye may,*" says he, "*and I'll sing ye a song tu.*" Of course he spoke with an Irish brogue. Of course he had been in the army. In ten minutes he pulled out an Army Agent's account, whereon his name was written. A few months after we read of him in a police court. How had I come to know him, to divine him ? Nothing shall convince me that I have not seen that man in the world of spirits. In the world of spirits and water I know I did : but that is a mere quibble of words. I was not surprised when he spoke in an Irish brogue. I had had cognizance of him before somehow. Who has not felt that little shock which arises when a person, a place, some words in a book (there is always a collocation) present themselves to you, and you know that you have before met the same person, words, scene, and so forth ?

They used to call the good Sir Walter the " Wizard of the North." What if some writer should appear who can write so *enchantingly* that he shall be able to call into actual life the people whom he invents ? What if Mignon, and Margaret, and Goetz von Berlichingen are alive now (though I don't say they are visible), and Dugald Dalgetty and Ivanhoe were to step in at that open window by the little garden yonder ? Suppose Uncas and our noble old Leather Stocking were to glide silent in ? Suppose Athos, Porthos, and Aramis should enter with a noiseless swagger, curling their moustaches ? And dearest Amelia Booth, on Uncle Toby's arm ; and Tittlebat Titmouse, with his hair dyed green ; and all the Crummles company of comedians, with the Gil Blas troop ; and Sir Roger de Coverley ; and the greatest of all crazy gentlemen, the Knight of La Mancha, with his blessed squire ? I say to you, I look rather wistfully towards the window, musing upon these people. Were any of them to enter, I think I should not be very much frightened. Dear old friends, what pleasant hours I have had with them ! We do not see each other very often, but when we do, we are ever happy to meet. I had a capital half-hour with Jacob Faithful last night ; when the last sheet was corrected, when "Finis" had been written, and the printer's boy, with the copy, was safe in Green Arbor Court.

So you are gone, little printer's boy, with the last scratches and corrections on the proof, and a fine flourish by way of Finis at the story's end. The last corrections? I say those last corrections seem never to be finished. A plague upon the weeds! Every day, when I walk in my own little literary garden-plot, I spy some, and should like to have a spud, and root them out. Those idle words, neighbor, are past remedy. That turning back to the old pages produces anything but elation of mind. Would you not pay a pretty fine to be able to cancel some of them? Oh, the sad old pages, the dull old pages! Oh, the cares, the *ennui*, the squabbles, the repetitions, the old conversations over and over again! But now and again a kind thought is recalled, and now and again a dear memory. Yet a few chapters more, and then the last : after which, behold Finis itself come to an end, and the Infinite begun.

AUTOUR DE MON CHAPEAU.

NEVER have I seen a more noble tragic face. In the centre of the forehead there was a great furrow of care, towards which the brows rose piteously. What a deep solemn grief in the eyes! They looked blankly at the object be-fore them, but through it, as it were, and into the grief beyond. In moments of pain, have you not looked at some indifferent object so? It mingles dumbly with your grief, and remains afterwards connected with it in your mind. It may be some indifferent thing — a book you were reading at the time when you received her farewell letter (how well you remember the paragraph afterwards — the shape of the words, and their position on the page); the words you were writing when your mother came in, and said it was all over — she was MARRIED — Emily married — to that insignificant little rival at whom you have laughed a hundred times in her company. Well, well; my friend and reader, whoe'er you be — old man or young, wife or maiden — you have had your grief-pang. Boy, you have lain awake the first night at school, and thought of home. Worse still, man, you have parted from the dear ones

with bursting heart : and, lonely boy, recall the
bolstering an unfeeling comrade gave you ; and,
lonely man just torn from your children — their
little tokens of affection yet in your pocket —
pacing the deck at evening in the midst of the
roaring ocean, you can remember how you were
told that supper was ready, and how you went
down to the cabin and had brandy-and-water
and biscuit. You remember the taste of them.
Yes ; forever. You took them whilst you and
your Grief were sitting together, and your Grief
clutched you round the soul. Serpent, how you
have writhed round me, and bitten me. Remorse, Remembrance, etc., come in the night
season, and I feel you gnawing, gnawing ! . . .
I tell you that man's face was like Laocoön's
(which, by the way, I always think over-rated.
The real head is at Brussels, at the Duke
Daremberg's, not at Rome).

That man ! What man ? That man of
whom I said that his magnificent countenance
exhibited the noblest tragic woe. He was not
of European blood. He was handsome, but not
of European beauty. His face white — not of
a northern whiteness ; his eyes protruding somewhat and rolling in their grief. Those eyes
had seen the Orient sun, and his beak was the
eagle's. His lips were full. The beard, curl-

ing round them, was unkempt and tawny. The
locks were of a deep, deep coppery red. The
hands, swart and powerful, accustomed to the
rough grasp of the wares in which he dealt,
seemed unused to the flimsy artifices of the
bath. He came from the Wilderness, and its
sands were on his robe, his cheek, his tattered
sandal, and the hardy foot it covered.

And his grief — whence came his sorrow? I
will tell you. He bore it in his hand. He had
evidently just concluded the compact by which
it became his. His business was that of a purchaser of domestic raiment. At early dawn —
nay, at what hour when the city is alive — do
we not all hear the nasal cry of " Clo "? In
Paris, *Habits Galons, Marchand d'habits*, is the
twanging signal with which the wandering merchant makes his presence known. It was in
Paris I saw this man. Where else have I not
seen him? In the Roman Ghetto — at the
Gate of David, in his fathers' once imperial
city. The man I mean was an itinerant vender
and purchaser of wardrobes — what you call an
. . . Enough! You know his name.

On his left shoulder hung his bag; and he
held in that hand a white hat, which I am sure
he had just purchased and which was the cause
of the grief which smote his noble features. Of

course I cannot particularize the sum, but he
had given too much for that hat. He felt he
might have got the thing for less money. It
was not the amount, I am sure ; it was the
principle involved. He had given fourpence
(let us say) for that which threepence would
have purchased. He had been done : and a
manly shame was upon him, that he, whose
energy, acuteness, experience, point of honor,
should have made him the victor in any mercantile duel in which he should engage, had
been overcome by a porter's wife, who very
likely sold him the old hat, or by a student
who was tired of it. I can understand his
grief. Do I seem to be speaking of it in a dis-
respectful or flippant way ? Then you mistake
me. He had been outwitted. He had desired,
coaxed, schemed, haggled, got what he wanted,
and now found he had paid too much for his
bargain. You don't suppose I would ask you
to laugh at that man's grief ? It is you,
clumsy cynic, who are disposed to sneer, whilst
it may be tears of genuine sympathy are trick-
ling down this nose of mine. What do you
mean by laughing ? If you saw a wounded
soldier on the field of battle, would you laugh ?
If you saw a ewe robbed of her lamb, would
you laugh, you brute ? It is you who are the

cynic, and have no feeling : and you sneer
because that grief is unintelligible to you
which touches my finer sensibility. The OLD-
CLOTHES-MAN had been defeated in one of the
daily battles of his most interesting, checkered,
adventurous life.

Have you ever figured to yourself what such
a life must be ? The pursuit and conquest of
twopence must be the most eager and fascinating of occupations. We might all engage in
that business if we would. Do not whist-players, for example, toil, and think, and lose their
temper over sixpenny points ? They bring
study, natural genius, long forethought, memory, and careful historical experience to bear
upon their favorite labor. Don't tell me that
it is the sixpenny points, and five shillings the
rub, which keeps them for hours over their
painted pasteboard. It is the desire to conquer. Hours pass by. Night glooms. Dawn,
it may be, rises unheeded ; and they sit calling
for fresh cards at the " Portland," or the
" Union," while waning candles splutter in the
sockets, and languid waiters snooze, in the ante-
room. Sol rises. Jones has lost four pounds :
Brown has won two ; Robinson lurks away to
his family house and (mayhap indignant) Mrs.
R. Hours of evening, night, morning, have

passed away whilst they have been waging this sixpenny battle. What is the loss of four pounds to Jones, the gain of two to Brown? B. is, perhaps, so rich that two pounds more or less are as naught to him ; J. is so hopelessly involved that to win four pounds cannot benefit his creditors, or alter his condition ; but they play for that stake : they put forward their best energies : they ruff, finesse (what are the technical words, and how do I know ?). It is but a sixpenny game if you like ; but they want to win it. So as regards my friend yonder with the hat. He stakes his money : he wishes to win the game, not the hat merely. I am not prepared to say that he is not inspired by a noble ambition. Cæsar wished to be first in a village. If first of a hundred yokels, why not first of two? And my friend the old-clothes-man wishes to win his game, as well as to turn his little sixpence.

Suppose in the game of life — and it is but a twopenny game after all — you are equally eager of winning. Shall you be ashamed of your ambition, or glory in it? There are games, too, which are becoming to particular periods of life. I remember in the days of our youth, when my friend Arthur Bowler was an eminent cricketer. Slim, swift, strong, well-built, he presented a goodly appearance on the ground in his flannel uniform. *Militâsti non sine gloria*, Bowler my boy! Hush! We tell no tales. Mum is the word. Yonder comes Charley his son. Now Charley his son has taken the field and is famous among the eleven of his school. Bowler senior, with his capacious waistcoat, etc., waddling after a ball, would present an absurd object, whereas it does the eyes good to see Bowler junior scouring the plain — a young exemplar of joyful health, vigor, activity. The old boy wisely contents himself with amusements more becoming his age and waist; takes his sober ride; visits his farm soberly — busies himself about his pigs, his ploughing, his peaches, or what not? Very small *routinier* amusements interest him; and (thank goodness!) nature provides very kindly for kindly-disposed fogies. We relish those things which we scorned in our lusty youth. I see the young folks of an evening kindling and glowing over their delicious novels. I look up and watch the eager eye flashing down the page, being, for my part, perfectly contented with my twaddling old volume of *Howel's Letters*, or the *Gentleman's Magazine*. I am actually arrived at such a calm frame of mind that I like batter-pudding. I never should have believed it possible ; but it is so. Yet a little while, and I may relish water-gruel. It will be the age of *mon lait de poule et mon bonnet de nuit.* And then — the cotton extinguisher is pulled over the old noddle, and the little flame of life is popped out.

Don't you know elderly people who make learned notes in Army Lists, Peerages, and the like ? This is the batter-pudding, water-gruel of old age. The worn-out old digestion does not care for stronger food. Formerly it could swallow twelve hours' tough reading, and digest an encyclopædia.

If I had children to educate, I would, at ten or twelve years of age, have a professor, or professoress, of whist for them, and cause them to be well grounded in that great and useful game. You cannot learn it well when you are old, any more than you can learn dancing or billiards. In our house at home we youngsters did not play whist because we were dear obedient children, and the elders said playing at cards was "a waste of time." A waste of time, my good people ! *Allons !* What do elderly home-keeping people do of a night after dinner ? Darby gets his newspaper ; my dear Joan her *Missionary Magazine* or her volume of Cumming's Sermons — and don't you know what ensues? Over the arm of Darby's arm-chair the paper flutters to the ground unheeded, and he performs the trumpet obligato *que vous savez* on his old nose. My dear old Joan's head nods over her sermon (awakening though the doctrine may be). Ding, ding, ding : can that be ten o'clock? It is time to send the servants to bed, my dear — and to bed master and mistress go too. But they have not wasted their time playing at cards. Oh, no! I belong to a Club where there is whist of a night; and not a little amusing is it to hear Brown speak of Thompson's play, and *vice versa*. But there is one man — Greatorex let us call him — who is the acknowledged captain and primus of all the whist-players. We all secretly admire him. I, for my part, watch him in private life, hearken to what he says, note what he orders for dinner, and have that feeling of awe for him that I used to have as a boy for the cock of the school. Not play at whist? *" Quelle triste vieillesse vous vous préparez !"* were the words of the great and good Bishop of Autun. I can't. It is too late now. Too late! too late! Ah! humiliating confession! That joy might have been clutched, but the life-stream has swept us by it — the swift life-stream rushing to the nearing sea. Too late! too late!

Twentystone my boy ! when you read in the papers " *Valse à deux temps*," and all the fashionable dances taught to adults by "Miss Lightfoots," don't you feel that you would like to go in and learn ?   Ah, it is too late !   You have passed the *choreas*, Master Twentystone, and the young people are dancing without you.

I don't believe much of what my Lord Byron the poet says ; but when he wrote, "So for a good old gentlemanly vice, I think I shall put up with avarice," I think his lordship meant what he wrote, and if he practiced what he preached, shall not quarrel with him.   As an occupation in declining years, I declare I think saving is useful, amusing, and not unbecoming. It must be a perpetual amusement.   It is a game that can be played by day, by night, at home and abroad, and at which you must win in the long run.   I am tired and want a cab. The fare to my house, say, is two shillings. The cabman will naturally want half a crown. I pull out my book.   I show him the distance is exactly three miles and fifteen hundred and ninety yards.   I offer him my card — my winning card.   As he retires with the two shillings, blaspheming inwardly, every curse is a compliment to my skill.   I have played him and beat him ; and a sixpence is my spoil and just reward.

This is a game, by the way, which women play far more cleverly than we do. But what an interest it imparts to life ! During the whole drive home I know I shall have my game at the journey's end ; am sure of my hand, and shall beat my adversary. Or I can play in another way. I won't have a cab at all, I will wait for the omnibus : I will be one of the damp fourteen in that steaming vehicle. I will wait about in the rain for an hour, and 'bus after 'bus shall pass, but I will not be beat. I *will* have a place, and get it at length, with my boots wet through, and an umbrella dripping between my legs. I have a rheumatism, a cold, a sore throat, a sulky evening, — a doctor's bill to-morrow, perhaps ? Yes, but I have won my game, and am gainer of a shilling on this rubber.

If you play this game all through life it is wonderful what daily interest it has, and amusing occupation. For instance, my wife goes to sleep after dinner over her volume of sermons. As soon as the dear soul is sound asleep, I advance softly and puff out her candle. Her pure dreams will be all the happier without that light ; and, say she sleeps an hour, there is a penny gained.

As for clothes, *parbleu !* there is not much

money to be saved in clothes, for the fact is, as a man advances in life — as he becomes an *Ancient Briton* (mark the pleasantry) — he goes without clothes. When my tailor proposes something in the way of a change of raiment, I laugh in his face. My blue coat and brass buttons will last these ten years. It is seedy? What then? I don't want to charm anybody in particular. You say that my clothes are shabby? What do I care? When I wished to look well in somebody's eyes, the matter may have been different. But now, when I receive my bill of 10*l.* (let us say) at the year's end, and contrast it with old tailors' reckonings, I feel that I have played the game with master tailor, and beat him ; and my old clothes are a token of the victory.

I do not like to give servants board-wages, though they are cheaper than household bills : but I know they save out of board-wages, and so beat me. This shows that it is not the money but the game which interests me. So about wine. I have it good and dear. I will trouble you to tell me where to get it good and cheap. You may as well give me the address of a shop where I can buy meat for fourpence a pound, or sovereigns for fifteen shillings apiece. At the game of auctions, docks, shy wine-merchants,

depend on it there is *no* winning ; and I would
as soon think of buying jewelry at an auction
in Fleet Street as of purchasing wine from one
of your dreadful needy wine-agents such as
infest every man's door.   Grudge myself good
wine ? As soon grudge my horse corn.   *Merci !*
that would be a very losing game indeed, and
your humble servant has no relish for such.

But in the very pursuit of saving there must
be a hundred harmless delights and pleasures
which we who are careless necessarily forego.
What do you know about the natural history of
your household ?   Upon your honor and conscience, do you know the price of a pound of
butter ?   Can you say what sugar costs, and
how much your family consumes and ought to
consume ?   How much lard do you use in your
house ?   As I think on these subjects I own I
hang down the head of shame.   I suppose for
a moment that you, who are reading this, are
a middle-aged gentleman, and paterfamilias.
Can you answer the above questions ?   You
know, sir, you cannot.   Now turn round, lay
down the book, and suddenly ask Mrs. Jones
and your daughters if *they* can answer ?   They
cannot.   They look at one another.   They pre-
tend they can answer.   They can tell you the
plot and principal characters of the last novel.

Some of them know something about history, geology, and so forth. But of the natural history of home — *Nichts,* and for shame on you all ! *Honnis soyez!* For shame on you! for shame on us !

In the early morning I hear a sort of call or *jodel* under my window : and know 't is the matutinal milkman leaving his can at my gate. O household gods ! have I lived all these years and don't know the price or the quantity of the milk which is delivered in that can ? Why don't I know ? As I live, if I live till to-morrow morning, as soon as I hear the call of Lactantius, I will dash out upon him. How many cows ? How much milk, on an average, all the year round ? What rent ? What cost of food and dairy servants ? What loss of animals, and average cost of purchase ? If I interested myself properly about my pint (or hogshead, whatever it be) of milk, all this knowledge would ensue ; all this additional interest in life. What is this talk of my friend, Mr. Lewes, about objects at the seaside, and so forth ?[1] Objects at the seaside ? Objects at the area-bell : objects before my nose : objects which the butcher brings me in his tray : which the cook dresses and puts down before me, and

[1] *Seaside Studies.* By G. H. Lewes.

over which I say grace ! My daily life is surrounded with objects which ought to interest me. The pudding I eat (or refuse, that is neither here nor there ; and, between ourselves, what I have said about batter-pudding may be taken *cum grano* — we are not come to *that* yet, except for the sake of argument or illustration) — the pudding, I say, on my plate, the eggs that made it, the fire that cooked it, the tablecloth on which it is laid, and so forth — are each and all of these objects a knowledge of which I may acquire — a knowledge of the cost and production of which I might advantageously learn. To the man who *does* know these things, I say the interest of life is prodigiously increased. The milkman becomes a study to him ; the baker a being he curiously and tenderly examines. Go, Lewes, and clap a hideous sea-anemone into a glass : I will put a cabman under mine, and make a vivisection of a butcher. O Lares, Penates, and gentle household gods, teach me to sympathize with all that comes within my doors ! Give me an interest in the butcher's book. Let us look forward to the ensuing number of the grocer's account with eagerness. It seems ungrateful to my kitchen-chimney not to know the cost of sweeping it ; and I trust that many a man who reads this, and muses on it, will feel, like the writer, ashamed of himself, and hang down his head humbly.

Now, if to this household game you could add a little money interest, the amusement would be increased far beyond the mere money value, as a game at cards for sixpence is better than a rubber for nothing. If you can interest yourself about sixpence, all life is invested with a new excitement. From sunrise to sleeping you can always be playing that game — with butcher, baker, coal-merchant, cabman, omnibus man — nay, diamond merchant and stock-broker. You can bargain for a guinea over the price of a diamond necklace, or for a sixteenth per cent. in a transaction at the Stock Exchange. We all know men who have this faculty who are not ungenerous with their money. They give it on great occasions. They are more able to help than you and I who spend ours, and say to poor Prodigal who comes to us out at elbow, "My dear fellow, I should have been delighted; but I have already anticipated my quarter, and am going to ask Screwby if he can do anything for me."

In this delightful, wholesome, ever-novel twopenny game, there is a danger of excess, as there is in every other pastime or occupation of life. If you grow too eager for your two-pence, the acquisition or the loss of it may affect your peace of mind, and peace of mind is better than any amount of twopences. My friend, the old-clothes'-man, whose agonies over the hat have led to this rambling disquisition, has, I very much fear, by a too eager pursuit of small profits, disturbed the equanimity of a mind that ought to be easy and happy. "Had I stood out," he thinks, "I might have had the hat for threepence," and he doubts whether, having given fourpence for it, he will ever get back his money. My good Shadrach, if you go through life passionately deploring the irrev-ocable, and allow yesterday's transactions to embitter the cheerfulness of to-day and to-mor-row — as lief walk down to the Seine, souse in, hats, body, clothes-bag and all, and put an end to your sorrow and sordid cares. Before and since Mr. Franklin wrote his pretty apologue of the Whistle have we not all made bargains of which we repented, and coveted and acquired objects for which we have paid too dearly! Who has not purchased his hat in some market or other? There is General McClellan's cocked hat for example; I dare say he was eager enough to wear it, and he has learned that it is by no means cheerful wear. There were the

military beavers of Messeigneurs of Orleans : [1]
they wore them gallantly in the face of battle ;
but I suspect they were glad enough to pitch
them into the James River and come home in
mufti. Ah, *mes amis! à chacun son schakot!*
I was looking at a bishop the other day, and
thinking, "My right reverend lord, that broad-
brim and rosette must bind your great broad
forehead very tightly, and give you many a
headache. A good easy wideawake were better for you, and I would like to see that honest
face with a cutty-pipe in the middle of it."
There is my Lord Mayor. My once dear lord,
my kind friend, when your two years' reign
was over, did you not jump for joy and fling
your cheapeau-bras out of window : and has n't
that hat cost you a pretty bit of money ?
There, in a splendid traveling chariot, in the
sweetest bonnet, all trimmed with orange-blos-
soms and Chantilly lace, sits my Lady Rosa,
with old Lord Snowden by her side. Ah, Rosa!
what a price have you paid for that hat which
you wear ! and is your ladyship's coronet not
purchased too dear ? Enough of hats. Sir, or
Madam, I take off mine, and salute you with
profound respect.

[1] Two cadets of the House of Orleans who served as Volunteers under General McClellan in his campaign against Rich-
mond.

THE LAST SKETCH.

Not many days since I went to visit a house where in former years I had received many a friendly welcome. We went into the owner's — an artist's — studio. Prints, pictures, and sketches hung on the walls as I had last seen and remembered them. The implements of the painter's art were there. The light which had shone upon so many, many hours of patient and cheerful toil poured through the northern window upon print and bust, lay figure and sketch, and upon the easel before which the good, the gentle, the beloved Leslie labored. In this room the busy brain had devised, and the skillful hand executed, I know not how many of the noble works which have delighted the world with their beauty and charming humor. Here the poet called up into pictorial presence, and informed with life, grace, beauty, infinite friendly mirth and wondrous naturalness of expression, the people of whom his dear books told him the stories, — his Shakespeare, his Cervantes, his Molière, his Le Sage. There was his last work on the easel — a beautiful fresh smiling shape of Titania, such as his sweet guileless fancy imagined the *Midsummer Night's*

queen to be. Gracious, and pure, and bright,
the sweet smiling image glimmers on the canvas. Fairy elves, no doubt, were to have been
grouped around their mistress in laughing clus-
ters. Honest Bottom's grotesque head and
form are indicated as reposing by the side of
the consummate beauty. The darkling forest
would have grown around them, with the stars
glittering from the midsummer sky ; the flowers at the queen's feet, and the boughs and
foliage about her, would have been peopled
with gamboling sprites and fays. They were
dwelling in the artist's mind, no doubt, and
would have been developed by that patient,
faithful, admirable genius : but the busy brain
stopped working, the skillful hand fell lifeless,
the loving, honest heart ceased to beat. What
was she to have been — that fair Titania —
when perfected by the patient skill of the poet,
who in imagination saw the sweet innocent
figure, and with tender courtesy and caresses,
as it were, posed and shaped and traced the
fair form ? Is there record kept anywhere
of fancies conceived, beautiful, unborn ? Some
day will they assume form in some yet unde-
veloped light ? If our bad unspoken thoughts
are registered against us, and are written in
the awful account, will not the good thoughts

unspoken, the love and tenderness, the pity,
beauty, charity, which pass through the breast,
and cause the heart to throb with silent good,
find a remembrance too ?   A few weeks more,
and this lovely offspring of the poet's concep-
tion would have been complete — to charm the
world with its beautiful mirth.   May there not
be some sphere unknown to us where it may
have an existence ?   They say our words, once
out of our lips, go traveling in *omne ævum,*
reverberating forever and ever.   If our words,
why not our thoughts ?   If the Has Been, why
not the Might Have Been ?

Some day our spirits may be permitted to
walk in galleries of fancies more wondrous and
beautiful than any achieved works which at
present we see, and our minds to behold and
delight in masterpieces which poets' and artists'
minds have fathered and conceived only.

With a feeling much akin to that with which
I looked upon the friend's — the admirable
artist's — unfinished work, I can fancy many
readers turning to the last pages which were
traced by Charlotte Brontë's hand.   Of the
multitude that have read her books, who has
not known and deplored the tragedy of her
family, her own most sad and untimely fate ?
Which of her readers has not become her

friend? Who that has known her books has not admired the artist's noble English, the burning love of truth, the bravery, the simplicity, the indignation at wrong, the eager sympathy, the pious love and reverence, the passionate honor, so to speak, of the woman? What a story is that of that family of poets in their solitude yonder on the gloomy northern moors! At nine o'clock at night, Mrs. Gaskell tells, after evening prayers, when their guardian and relative had gone to bed, the three poetesses — the three maidens, Charlotte, and Emily, and Anne — Charlotte being the "motherly friend and guardian to the other two" — "began, like restless wild animals, to pace up and down their parlor, 'making out' their wonderful stories, talking over plans and projects and thoughts of what was to be their future life."

One evening at the close of 1854, as Charlotte Nicholls sat with her husband by the fire, listening to the howling of the wind about the house, she suddenly said to her husband, "If you had not been with me, I must have been writing now." She then ran up stairs, and brought down, and read aloud, the beginning of a new tale. When she had finished, her husband remarked, "The critics will accuse you of repetition." She replied, "Oh! I shall alter that. I always begin two or three times before I can please myself." But it was not to be. The trembling little hand was to write no more. The heart newly awakened to love and happiness, and throbbing with maternal hope, was soon to cease to beat; that intrepid outspeaker and champion of truth, that eager, impetuous redresser of wrong, was to be called out of the world's fight and struggle, to lay down the shining arms, and to be removed to a sphere where even a noble indignation *cor ulterius nequit lacerare,* and where truth complete, and right triumphant, no longer need to wage war.

I can only say of this lady, *vidi tantum.* I saw her first just as I rose out of an illness from which I had never thought to recover. I remember the trembling little frame, the little hand, the great honest eyes. An impetuous honesty seemed to me to characterize the woman. Twice I recollect she took me to task for what she held to be errors in doctrine. Once about Fielding we had a disputation. She spoke her mind out. She jumped too rapidly to conclusions. (I have smiled at one or two passages in the *Biography,* in which my own disposition or behavior forms the subject of talk.)

She formed conclusions that might be wrong, and built whole theories of character upon them. New to the London world, she entered it with an independent, indomitable spirit of her own ; and judged of contemporaries, and especially spied out arrogance or affectation, with extraordinary keenness of vision. She was angry with her favorites if their conduct or conversation fell below her ideal. Often she seemed to me to be judging the London folk prematurely : but perhaps the city is rather angry at being judged. I fancied an austere little Joan of Arc marching in upon us, and rebuking our easy lives, our easy morals. She gave me the impression of being a very pure, and lofty, and high-minded person. A great and holy reverence of right and truth seemed to be with her always. Such, in our brief interview, she appeared to me. As one thinks of that life so noble, so lonely — of that passion for truth — of those nights and nights of eager study, swarming fancies, invention, depression, elation, prayer ; as one reads the necessarily incomplete though most touching and admirable history of the heart that throbbed in this one little frame — of this one amongst the myriads of souls that have lived and died on this great earth—this great earth?—this little speck

in the infinite universe of God, — with what wonder do we think of to-day, with what awe await
to-morrow, when that which is now but darkly
seen shall be clear ! As I read this little fragmentary sketch, I think of the rest. Is it ?
And where is it ? Will not the leaf be turned
some day, and the story be told ? Shall the
deviser of the tale somewhere perfect the history of little EMMA's griefs and troubles ?
Shall TITANIA come forth complete with her
sportive court, with the flowers at her feet, the
forest around her, and all the stars of summer
glittering overhead ?

How well I remember the delight, and
wonder, and pleasure with which I read *Jane
Eyre*, sent to me by an author whose name
and sex were then alike unknown to me ; the
strange fascinations of the book ; and how,
with my own work pressing upon me, I could
not, having taken the volumes up, lay them
down until they were read through ! Hundreds of those who, like myself, recognized and
admired that master-work of a great genius,
will look with a mournful interest and regard
and curiosity upon the last fragmentary sketch
from the noble hand which wrote *Jane Eyre*.

THE CURATE'S WALK.

I.

IT was the third out of the four bell-buttons at the door at which my friend the curate pulled; and the summons was answered after a brief interval.

I must premise that the house before which we stopped was No. 14, Sedan Buildings, leading out of Great Guelph Street, Dettingen Street, Culloden Street, Minden Square; and Upper and Lower Caroline Row form part of the same quarter — a very queer and solemn quarter to walk in, I think, and one which always suggests Fielding's novels to me. I can fancy Captain Booth strutting out of the very door at which we were standing, in tarnished lace, with his hat cocked over his eye, and his hand on his hanger; or Lady Bellaston's chair and bearers coming swinging down Great

Guelph Street, which we have just quitted to enter Sedan Buildings.

Sedan Buildings is a little flagged square, ending abruptly with the huge walls of Bluck's Brewery. The houses, by many degrees smaller than the large decayed tenements in Great Guelph Street, are still not uncomfortable, although shabby. There are brass-plates on the doors, two on some of them : or simple names as " Lunt," " Padgemore," etc. (as if no other statement about Lunt and Padgemore were necessary at all), under the bells. There are pictures of mangles before two of the houses, and a gilt arm with a hammer sticking out from one. I never saw a Goldbeater. What sort of a being is he, that he always sticks out his ensign in dark, mouldy, lonely, dreary, but somewhat respectable places? What powerful Mulciberian fellows they must be, those Goldbeaters, whacking and thumping with huge mallets at the precious metals all day. I wonder what is Goldbeaters' skin? and do they get impregnated with the metal? and are their great arms under their clean shirts on Sundays, all gilt and shining?

It is a quiet, kind, respectable place somehow, in spite of its shabbiness. Two pewter pints and a jolly little half-pint are hanging on

the railings in perfect confidence, basking in
what little sun comes into the Court. A group
of small children are making an ornament of
oyster-shells in one corner. Who has that
half-pint ? Is it for one of those small ones, or
for some delicate female recommended to take
beer ? The windows in the Court, upon some
of which the sun glistens, are not cracked, and
pretty clean ; it is only the black and dreary
look behind which gives them a poverty-stricken
appearance. No curtains or blinds. A bird-
cage and very few pots of flowers here and
there. This — with the exception of a milkman talking to a whity-brown woman, made up
of bits of flannel and strips of faded chintz and
calico seemingly, and holding a long bundle
which cried — this was all I saw in Sedan
Buildings while we were waiting until the door
should open.

At last the door was opened, and by a por-
teress so small, that I wonder how she ever
could have lifted up the latch. She bobbed a
courtesy, and smiled at the Curate, whose face
gleamed with benevolence too, in reply to that
salutation.

"Mother not at home ?" says Frank Whitestock, patting the child on the head.

"Mother 's out charing, sir," replied the

girl; "but please to walk up, sir." And she led the way up one and two pair of stairs to that apartment in the house which is called the second-floor front; in which was the abode of the charwoman.

There were two young persons in the room, of the respective ages of eight and five, I should think. She of five years of age was hemming a duster, being perched on a chair at the table in the middle of the room. The elder, of eight, politely wiped a chair with a cloth for the accommodation of the good-natured Curate, and came and stood between his knees, immediately alongside of his umbrella, which also reposed there, and which she by no means equaled in height.

"These children attend my school at St. Timothy's," Mr. Whitestock said, "and Betsy keeps the house while her mother is from home."

Anything cleaner or neater than this house it is impossible to conceive. There was a big bed, which must have been the resting-place of the whole of this little family. There were three or four religious prints on the walls; besides two framed and glazed, of Prince Coburg and the Princess Charlotte. There were brass candlesticks, and a lamb on the chimney-piece, and a cupboard in the corner, decorated with near half a dozen plates, yellow bowls, and crockery. And on the table there were two or three bits of dry bread, and a jug with water, with which these three young people (it being then nearly three o'clock) were about to take their meal called tea.

That little Betsy who looks so small is nearly ten years old : and has been a mother ever since the age of about five. I mean to say that her own mother having to go out upon her charing operations, Betsy assumes command of the room during her parent's absence : has nursed her sisters from babyhood up to the present time : keeps order over them, and the house clean as you see it ; and goes out occasionally and transacts the family purchases of bread, moist sugar, and mother's tea. They dine upon bread, tea and breakfast upon bread when they have it, or go to bed without a morsel. Their holiday is Sunday, which they spend at Church and Sunday-school. The younger children scarcely ever go out, save on that day, but sit sometimes in the sun, which comes in pretty pleasantly : sometimes blue in the cold, for they very seldom see a fire except to heat irons by, when mother has a job of linen to get up. Father was a journeyman

bookbinder, who died four years ago, and is
buried among thousands and thousands of the
nameless dead who lie crowding the black
churchyard of St. Timothy's parish.

The Curate evidently took especial pride in
Victoria, the youngest of these three children
of the charwoman, and caused Betsy to fetch a
book which lay at the window, and bade her
read.   It was a Missionary Register which the
Curate opened hap-hazard, and this baby began
to read out in an exceedingly clear and resolute
voice about —

"The island of Raritongo is the least fre-
quented of all the Caribbean Archipelago.
Wankyfungo is at four leagues S. E. by E., and
the peak of the crater of Shuagnahua is dis-
tinctly visible.   The 'Irascible' entered Rari-
tongo Bay on the evening of Thursday 29th,
and the next day the Rev. Mr. Flethers, Mrs.
Flethers, and their nine children, and Shang-
pooky, the native converted at Cacabawgo,
landed and took up their residence at the house
of Ratatatua, the principal Chief, who entertained us with yams and a pig," etc., etc., etc.

"Raritongo, Wankyfungo, Archipelago."   I
protest this little woman read off each of these
long words with an ease which perfectly astonished me.   Many a lieutenant in her Majesty's

Heavies would be puzzled with words half the length. Whitestock, by way of reward for her scholarship, gave her another pat on the head; having received which present with a courtesy, she went and put the book back into the window, and clambering back into the chair resumed the hemming of the blue duster.

I suppose it was the smallness of these people, as well as their singular, neat, and tidy behavior, which interested me so. Here were three creatures not so high as the table, with all the labors, duties, and cares of life upon their little shoulders, working and doing their duty like the biggest of my readers; regular, laborious, cheerful — content with small pittances, practicing a hundred virtues of thrift and order.

Elizabeth, at ten years of age, might walk out of this house and take the command of a small establishment. She can wash, get up linen, cook, make purchases, and buy bargains. If I were ten years old and three feet in height I would marry her, and we would go and live in a cupboard, and share the little half-pint pot for dinner. 'Melia, eight years of age, though inferior in accomplishments to her sister, is her equal in size, and can wash, scrub, hem, go errands, put her hand to the dinner, and make herself generally useful. In a word, she is fit to be a little housemaid, and to make everything but the beds, which she cannot as yet reach up to. As for Victoria's qualifications, they have been mentioned before. I wonder whether the Princess Alice can read off "Rari-tongo," etc., as glibly as this surprising little animal.

I asked the Curate's permission to make these young ladies a present, and accordingly produced the sum of sixpence to be divided amongst the three. "What will you do with it?" I said, laying down the coin.

They answered, all three at once, and in a little chorus, "We'll give it to mother." This verdict caused the disbursement of another sixpence, and it was explained to them that the sum was for their own private pleasures, and each was called upon to declare what she would purchase.

Elizabeth says, "I would like twopenn'orth of meat, if you please, sir."

'Melia: "Ha'porth of treacle, three-far-things'-worth of milk, and the same of fresh bread."

Victoria, speaking very quick, and gasping in an agitated manner: "Ha'pny — aha — orange, and ha'pny — aha — apple, and ha'pny

— aha — treacle, and — and " — here her imagination failed her. She did not know what to do with the rest of the money.

At this 'Melia actually interposed, " Suppose she and Victoria subscribed a farthing apiece out of their money, so that Betsy might have a quarter of a pound of meat ? " She added that her sister wanted it, and that it would do her good. Upon my word, she made the proposal and the calculations in an instant, and all of her own accord. And before we left them, Betsy had put on the queerest little black shawl and bonnet, and had a mug and a basket ready to receive the purchases in question.

Sedan Buildings has a particularly friendly look to me since that day. Peace be with you, O thrifty, kindly, simple, loving, little maidens ! May their voyage in life prosper ! Think of the great journey before them, and the little cock-boat manned by babies venturing over the great stormy ocean.

II.

FOLLOWING the steps of little Betsy with her mug and basket, as she goes pattering down the street, we watch her into a grocer's shop, where a startling placard with " DOWN

AGAIN !" written on it announces that the
Sugar Market is still in a depressed condition
—and where she no doubt negotiates the purchase of a certain quantity of molasses. A
little further on, in Lawfeldt Street, is Mr.
Filch's fine silversmith's shop, where a man
may stand for a half-hour and gaze with rav-
ishment at the beautiful gilt cups and tank-
ards, the stunning waistcoat chains, the little
white cushions laid out with delightful diamond
pins, gold horseshoes and splinter-bars, pearl
owls, turquoise lizards and dragons, enameled
monkeys, and all sorts of agreeable monsters
for your neck-cloth. If I live to be a hundred,
or if the girl of my heart were waiting for me
at the corner of the street, I never could pass
Mr. Filch's shop without having a couple of
minutes' good stare at the window. I like to
fancy myself dressed up in some of the jewelry.
"Spec, you rogue," I say, "suppose you were
to get leave to wear three or four of those
rings on your fingers ; to stick that opal, round
which twists a brilliant serpent with a ruby
head, into your blue satin neck-cloth ; and to
sport that gold jack-chain on your waistcoat.
You might walk in the Park with that black
whalebone prize-riding-whip, which has a head
the size of a snuff-box, surmounted with a sil-

ver jockey on a silver race-horse ; and what a sensation you would create, if you took that large ram's horn with the cairngorm top out of your pocket, and offered a pinch of rappee to the company round !'' A little attorney's clerk is staring in at the window, in whose mind very similar ideas are passing. What would he not give to wear that gold pin next Sunday in his blue hunting neck-cloth? The ball of it is almost as big as those which are painted over the side door of Mr. Filch's shop, which is down that passage which leads into Trotter's Court.

I have dined at a house where the silver dishes and covers came from Filch's, let out to their owner by Mr. Filch for the day, and in charge of the grave-looking man whom I mistook for the butler. Butlers and ladies'-maids innumerable have audiences of Mr. Filch in his back-parlor. There are suits of jewels which he and his shop have known for a half-century past, so often have they been pawned to him. When we read in the *Court Journal* of Lady Fitzball's head-dress of lappets and superb diamonds, it is because the jewels get a day rule from Filch's, and come back to his iron box as soon as the drawing-room is over. These jewels become historical among pawnbrokers. It was here that Lady Prigsby brought her diamonds one evening of last year, and desired hurriedly to raise two thousand pounds upon them, when Filch respectfully pointed out to her ladyship that she had pawned the stones already to his comrade, Mr. Tubal, of Charing Cross. And, taking his hat, and putting the case under his arm, he went with her ladyship to the hack-cab in which she had driven to Lawfeldt Street, entered the vehicle with her, and they drove in silence to the back entrance of her mansion in Monmouth Square, where Mr. Tubal's young man was still seated in the hall, waiting until her ladyship should be undressed.

We walked round the splendid shining shop and down the passage, which would be dark but that the gas-lit door is always swinging to and fro, as the people who come to pawn go in and out. You may be sure there is a gin-shop handy to all pawnbrokers'.

A lean man in a dingy dress is walking lazily up and down the flags of Trotter's Court. His ragged trousers trail in the slimy mud there. The doors of the pawnbroker's, and of the gin-shop on the other side, are banging to and fro : a little girl comes out of the former, with a tattered old handkerchief, and goes up and gives something to the dingy man. It is ninepence, just raised on his waistcoat. The man bids the child to "cut away home," and when she is clear out of the court, he looks at us with a lurking scowl and walks into the gin-shop doors, which swing always opposite the pawnbroker's shop.

Why should he have sent the waistcoast wrapped in that ragged old cloth? Why should he have sent the child into the pawnbroker's box, and not have gone himself? He did not choose to let her see him go into the gin-shop —why drive her in at the opposite door? The child knows well enough whither he is gone. She might as well have carried an old waistcoat in her hand through the street as a ragged napkin. A sort of vanity, you see, drapes itself in that dirty rag; or is it a kind of debauched shame, which does not like to go naked? The fancy can follow the poor girl up the black alley, up the black stairs, into the bare room, where mother and children are starving, while the lazy ragamuffin, the family bully, is gone into the gin-shop to "try our celebrated Cream of the Valley," as the bill in red letters bids him.

"I waited in this court the other day," Whitestock said, "just like that man, while a

friend of mine went in to take her husband's
tools out of pawn — an honest man — a journeyman shoemaker, who lives hard by." And
we went to call on the journeyman shoemaker
— Randle's Buildings — two-pair back — over
a blacking manufactory. The blacking was
made by one manufactor, who stood before a
tub stirring up his produce, a good deal of
which — and nothing else — was on the floor.
We passed through this emporium, which abut-
ted on a dank, steaming little court, and up the
narrow stair to the two-pair back.

The shoemaker was at work with his recov-
ered tools, and his wife was making women's
shoes (an inferior branch of the business) by
him. A shriveled child was lying on the bed
in the corner of the room. There was no bedstead, and indeed scarcely any furniture, save
the little table on which lay his tools and shoes
— a fair-haired, lank, handsome young man,
with a wife who may have been pretty once, in
better times, and before starvation pulled her
down. She had but one thin gown; it clung to
a frightfully emaciated little body.

Their story was the old one. The man had
been in good work, and had the fever. The
clothes had been pawned, the furniture and
bedstead had been sold, and they slept on the

mattress; the mattress went, and they slept on
the floor; the tools went, and the end of all
things seemed at hand, when the gracious appa-
rition of the Curate with his umbrella came and
cheered those stricken-down poor folks.

The journeyman shoemaker must have been
astonished at such a sight.   He is not, or was
not, a church-goer.   He is a man of "advanced"
opinions; believing that priests are hypocrites,
and that clergymen in general drive about in
coaches-and-four, and eat a tithe-pig a day.
This proud priest got Mr. Crispin a bed to lie
upon, and some soup to eat; and (being the
treasurer of certain good folks of his parish,
whose charities he administers), as soon as the
man was strong enough to work, the Curate
lent him money wherewith to redeem his tools,
and which our friend is paying back by install-
ments at this day.   And any man who has seen
these two honest men talking together would
have said the shoemaker was the haughtiest of
the two.

We paid one more morning visit.   This was
with an order for work to a tailor of reduced
circumstances and enlarged family.   He had
been a master, and was now forced to take
work by the job.   He who had commanded
many men was now fallen down to the ranks

again. His wife told us all about his misfortunes. She is evidently very proud of them. "He failed for seven thousand pounds," the poor woman said, three or four times during the course of our visit. It gave her husband a sort of dignity to have been trusted for so much money.

The Curate must have heard that story many times to which he now listened with great patience in the tailor's house — a large, clean, dreary, faint-looking room, smelling of poverty. Two little stunted, yellow-headed children, with lean pale faces and large protruding eyes, were at the window staring with all their might at Guy Fawkes, who was passing in the street, and making a great clattering and shouting outside, while the luckless tailor's wife was prating within about her husband's by-gone riches. I shall not in a hurry forget the picture. The empty room in a dreary background; the tailor's wife in brown, stalking up and down the planks, talking endlessly; the solemn children staring out of the window as the sunshine fell on their faces, and honest Whitestock seated, listening, with the tails of his coat through the chair.

His business over with the tailor, we start again. Frank Whitestock trips through alley after alley, never getting any mud on his boots, somehow, and his white neckcloth making a wonderful shine in those shady places. He has all sorts of acquaintance, chiefly amongst the extreme youth, assembled at the doors or about the gutters. There was one small person occupied in emptying one of these rivulets with an oyster-shell, for the purpose, apparently, of making an artificial lake in a hole hard by, whose solitary gravity and business air struck me much, while the Curate was very deep in conversation with a small coalman. A half dozen of her comrades were congregated round a scraper and on a grating hard by, playing with a mangy little puppy, the property of the Curate's friend.

I know it is wrong to give large sums of money away promiscuously, but I could not help dropping a penny into the child's oyster-shell, as she came forward holding it before her like a tray. At first her expression was one rather of wonder than of pleasure at this influx of capital, and was certainly quite worth the small charge of one penny, at which it was purchased.

For a moment she did not seem to know what steps to take ; but, having communed in her own mind, she presently resolved to turn them towards a neighboring apple-stall, in the direction of which she went without a single word of compliment passing between us. Now, the children round the scraper were witnesses to the transaction. " He 's give her a penny," one remarked to another, with hopes miserably disappointed that they might come in for a similar present.

She walked on to the apple-stall meanwhile, holding her penny behind her. And what did the other little ones do? They put down the puppy as if it had been so much dross. And one after another they followed the penny-piece to the apple-stall.